PONIES AT THE POINT

The ponies emerged from the dark cave, stepping into the daylight with a toss of the head or a quick kick of the heels. Mandy gestured to James to come and see.

James took the coil of rope from his shoulder and stood poised to throw it.

'Here come Rosie and Connie.' Mandy saw that the mare and her foal were the last to leave the cave. Now Rosie was sniffing the air with her flaring nostrils, her ears flicking this way and that.

'Has she spotted us?' James drew back quickly and pressed against the rock.

Mandy kept her nerve and stayed where she was. 'Maybe. But they have to come this way. Stand by, James!'

Animal Ark series

LUCY DANIELS

Ponies
— *at the* —
Point

Illustrations by Jenny Gregory

Hodder
Children's
Books

a division of Hodder Headline plc

Special thanks to Jenny Oldfield
Thanks also to C. J. Hall, B.Vet.Med., M.R.C.V.S., for reviewing
the veterinary information contained in this book.

Text copyright © 1998 Ben M. Baglio
Created by Ben M. Baglio, London W12 7QY
Illustrations copyright © 1998 Jenny Gregory

First published in Great Britain in 1998
by Hodder Children's Books

A Catalogue record for this book is available from the British Library

ISBN 0 340 72400 5

Typeset by Avon Dataset Ltd, Bidford-on-Avon, Warks

Printed and bound in Great Britain by
Clays Ltd, St Ives plc

Hodder Children's Books
a division of Hodder Headline plc
338 Euston Road
London NW1 3BH

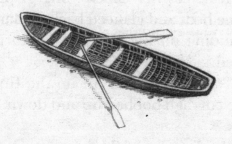

One

'Rather them than me!' Mandy Hope watched her mum and dad set out to sea in a boat which looked rather like a canoe.

'Yes, it doesn't look very safe.' James Hunter grinned as the strange boat rocked and dipped between the waves. One small fisherman's boat made from wood and tarred canvas against the might of the Atlantic Ocean.

'Hold tight!' Adam Hope yelled at his wife, above the roar of the water. He pulled sturdily at the oars.

'I *am* holding tight!' Emily Hope said with a

laugh. The wind caught her long red hair and whipped it across her cheeks. She gripped the sides of the boat and glanced back at Mandy and James standing on the shore. 'Your turn next!' she warned.

'Oh no!' Mandy backed off up the fine white sand. The curragh bobbed up and down. 'Maybe tomorrow.'

Today, the first day of their summer holiday in Connemara, was a day for exploring dry land. Here was the wild Ireland that the Hopes had looked forward to; cliffs and mountains, a ruined tower no longer lived in, but home no doubt to mice, bats and foxes; all fascinating to vets' daughter, Mandy Hope.

'Don't you fancy getting wet?' James asked with a grin. 'That's not like you, Mandy!'

Kicking her sandals off her feet and feeling the fine sand underfoot, she walked on. 'James, did you bother to stick a toe in that water?'

There was hundreds of miles of sea out there, beyond the rocky islets. When it came crashing on to Drumcashel beach, sending white spray curling over the black rocks, it was icy cold.

James paused. The wind tugged at his jacket

and blew the heavy brown fringe of hair back from his forehead. 'Your mum and dad might see seals,' he said quietly.

Mandy stopped and turned. 'Do you think so?'

He nodded. 'There's bound to be some out there.' Gazing out over Drumcashel Bay, he pointed to the rocks where seal colonies would have their haul-outs.

Mandy stared out across the semicircular bay. Seals swimming between the rocks, hauling their slippery grey bodies out of the water, basking in the sun. Seals with their wonderful, wide, dark eyes, their trusting natures. 'Mum!' she called. 'Dad, come back!' Suddenly she wanted to be out there with them in the fisherman's boat.

'. . . And basking sharks,' James went on, secretly smiling. 'And puffins and guillemots and shelducks . . .'

Mandy's voice was lost in the wind and the waves. Adam Hope rowed steadily out across the bay.

'. . . Oyster-catchers, gannets, gulls . . .'

'Stop!' Mandy was mad at herself. She'd missed a chance to see some of the animals and birds she loved.

'Never mind,' James teased. 'You've probably

got jet-lag from travelling here all the way from Yorkshire. That's why you're not your usual self.' He stooped to pick up a pure white scallop shell to add to the collection in the pocket of his fleece jacket.

'We came by ferry,' – across the Irish sea from Holyhead to Dublin, bringing her best friend, James, on holiday with them as usual – 'then car,' – a day's drive in Mrs Hope's four-wheel drive through green, damp countryside to the peat-bogs, lakes and mountains of Connemara. They'd passed Lough Caher and the mountains of Benmore, and found their whitewashed holiday cottage in the village of Drumcashel on the cliffs overlooking the sea. 'How could I possibly have jet-lag?'

Still annoyed with herself, Mandy gave up on the idea of getting her mum and dad to turn back. Instead, she headed into the first of several narrow coves that cut into the wider sweep of the bay. She looked up at the sheer rocks rising to either side, then down at the smooth, firm sand. 'Let's look for crabs in the rock-pools,' she suggested.

James watched her sprint ahead. He pulled a local map out of another pocket. 'Would you like to know what this cove is called?' he yelled after her.

'Yeah, sure.' Mandy scrambled on to the nearest rocks and crouched over a clear pool. Fronds of green seaweed waved in the water. Tiny silver fish darted for the cover of an overhanging slab of rock. The pool smelled salty and fishy; an exciting seaside smell.

James followed slowly, studying the map. 'This first one is Cashel Cove, with the castle up there on the headland.' He pointed to the crumbling grey ruin with a tall round tower overlooking the sea. There was no roof, and the walls were battered by the wind and rain. 'The next one along is called Kilmore Cove; I expect there's a church around here somewhere.'

James had been learning about Irish place names. He knew that *cashel* meant castle, and *kil* meant church.

'There's loads more to explore, Mandy!' Inishdrum and Inishdun were islands off the mainland, then there were Keem Point and Killala Bay further along the coast.

'Yeah!' She was on her hands and knees, staring at a tiny, see-through crab that crawled slowly over the bottom of the pool, trawling for food with his

pincer-claws. She let James wander on alone.

'Hey!' He rounded the next pointed headland and came running back. 'Mandy, come and look! Footprints in the sand! No, I mean *hoof*prints! Hundreds of them!'

'Hundreds?' Mandy jumped up. She left the crab to its silent world, jumped down on to the sand and raced to join James. 'What kind of hoofprints?' What animals did they have round here? Drumcashel was a fishing village; one main street with twenty or thirty houses, one shop-cum-pub, and a few farms scattered on the outskirts.

Could the prints have been made by cows, or sheep, or even goats?

'Ponies!' James sprinted back into Kilmore Cove. Then he stopped dead. A herd of ponies had suddenly appeared on the beach while he was away fetching Mandy.

'Ponies!' she echoed.

The animals turned their heads to gaze at the intruders, flicking their ears and stamping their feet. They were all different colours, grey, dun, black, bay and brown. As the wind blew spray off the sea, the ponies were shrouded in mist, like shadows that might melt away. But when the air cleared, they were still there, solid and silent, twitching their long tails and turning their heads away again.

'Beautiful!' Mandy breathed. She counted over twenty ponies standing on the beach, noted their small, neat heads, their short, strong legs. They had large eyes and long manes, and they looked from their wary glances and alert stance as if no man had ever gone near them.

'Are they wild?' James seemed to echo Mandy's thought.

'It looks like it. They're not wearing headcollars.' She stared hard through the spray which blew in again from the crashing waves. Almost without noticing, Mandy had crept closer for a better view.

The herd had begun to mill around the dead-end of the cove, pawing the ground and dipping their heads. One pony seemed to be in charge of keeping the others together in a tight bunch; a reddish-brown mare with white specks over her back and withers. She had a half-grown chestnut foal who followed in her shadow wherever she went.

Then, as the mare kept order in the herd, Mandy and James saw a young grey pony toss his head and break away. He kicked as he turned, landing one hoof against the flanks of a nearby piebald. The black and white pony gave a shrill protest.

Mandy gasped. She and James had approached to within fifty or so paces of the herd. But now they stopped.

The head of the herd blew down her nostrils; a warning snort to the young grey. She trotted smartly to him and gave him a sharp nip on the shoulder. The rebel pony lowered his head and retreated into the centre of the group.

James grinned. 'She told him off!'

'I bet that hurt!' Mandy whispered back. The mare's teeth had taken a real hold. 'Look at the way she's keeping us in her sights!' There was no doubt in her mind now that she and James had stumbled across unbroken ponies in the deserted cove. The herd was behaving exactly as any pack of wild animals would when strangers came upon them. She knew that they would keep close together, ready to flee if the danger came too near.

The strawberry roan mare circled her herd, shadowed by the chestnut foal. She lifted her feet high, stepping out with a free, easy action, flicking her ears towards Mandy and James whenever she changed direction.

'Where did they come from?' James couldn't get over the way the ponies had suddenly appeared. 'I saw the prints in the sand,' he insisted, 'but there was no sign of the actual ponies!'

'Maybe they were in that cave.' Mandy pointed to a dark arch of rock at the narrowest point in the cove. She glanced up at the cliffs above. 'There's no way they could have climbed down, anyway.'

Her heart beat fast as she watched the mare circle the outside of the herd. The other ponies jostled and turned on the spot, churning up the soft sand. She heard the thud of hooves, the whisk of tails against the further-off crash of the waves.

'Are we scaring them?' James asked. He drew back against a tall rock, out of the way.

Mandy nodded. 'They look as if they're getting ready to make a run for it.' She too stepped back, though she longed to move in closer. This was better than rock-pools or rowing out to sea in a curragh. Her eyes sparkled and she pushed her fair hair off her face as she gave the ponies room to move out of the cove.

The lead mare came round in a wider circle. Her dark-brown mane and tail streamed in the wind.

'Watch out!' James warned.

Now the whole herd of twenty ponies broke out of the tight knot by the overhanging cave entrance. They followed the lead mare in a straight charge down the beach, pounding their hooves into the sand.

Mandy took a deep breath as the ponies raced by. She saw the young chestnut foal tuck herself in behind her mother. The rebel grey was sandwiched between two bigger ponies, cantering shoulder to shoulder.

And then they were gone. The rush of swiftly moving bodies was over, the churned sand the only reminder that the wild ponies had ever gathered there in Kilmore Cove.

Two

'Do you know we're being watched?' James asked Mandy as they made their way along the beach.

The ponies had left their trail along the water's edge and were out of sight around the headland overlooked by the castle. As the tide came in, the waves would wash their hoofprints away.

'Where?' Mandy looked round with a start. She could see the small speck of the curragh by one of the rocky islands out to sea. Behind her, the cliffs rose almost sheer.

'From over there.' James pointed back the way they had walked. 'See that church up on the hill?'

She nodded. The square tower and arched windows of the sturdy building had just come into view. It perched on the cliff, surrounded by stone crosses in a small, grassy graveyard. 'I can't see anyone,' Mandy murmured. There were only the gulls wheeling across the windy sky.

'Look again. Past the church, right on the edge of the cliff.'

She squinted hard. As the spray from the waves spattered cold drops on her bare legs, Mandy made out the figure James was pointing at.

'See him?'

'Yep.' There was a boy standing there, looking down over Kilmore Cove. She could just pick him out, leaning against the largest stone cross, keeping her and James in his sight as they wandered along the beach. 'What's he staring at?'

James shrugged. 'It's like he's keeping guard.'

'Over what?'

'The ponies.' He frowned and turned his back on the unexpected sentry. 'I thought we said they were wild.'

'They are,' Mandy insisted. Ponies were like zebra and deer. They were flight animals who ran away when an attacker came near. That was exactly what the herd had just done. She stopped

James before he could speak again. 'Yes, I know, if the ponies don't have owners, why is the boy standing guard like that?'

'Exactly.' James didn't like being stared at. Of all the places that the boy could have chosen in this wide open countryside, he had to pick the spot where they were. 'And besides, do we know if there are any wild ponies left in Ireland?'

Mandy decided they couldn't do anything about the staring boy. She turned to catch up with James. 'Maybe there are wild ponies in this part of Connemara,' she suggested. 'Like on Exmoor in England. It's kind of a national park where they let the ponies roam free.' She liked the idea that there were such places. 'No towns, no roads . . .'

'No civilisation!' James agreed. He took a lungful of fresh sea air. 'A huge park where no one can build.'

'A park for wildlife.'

'For ponies!' Mandy grinned. It was a brilliant possibility. 'Let's find out!'

'I suppose there could still be wild ponies in Connemara,' Emily Hope agreed.

The Hopes and James were walking the winding road from their holiday cottage to the village on their first evening in Drumcashel. The minute Mandy's mum and dad had returned from their boat trip, too exhausted to cook for themselves, Adam Hope had promised to treat them all to supper at Molloys. Now, with huge appetites and lots to talk about, they were heading for the village pub-cum-grocery-store.

'What do you think, Dad?' Mandy asked.

'Well, if the ones you saw were true Connemaras, they would be roughly fourteen hands high, and sturdy enough to cope with the mountains and rough countryside round here.' He gestured towards the patchwork of fields, stretching towards peat-bogs and the mountains of Benmore in the distance. 'Connemaras can be any colour. They're hardy and very agile. Would your ones fit that description?'

'Exactly!' Mandy told her dad about the strong, sturdy-legged herd they'd seen.

'And intelligent,' Emily Hope added. Like Adam, her training at vet school had given her plenty of knowledge about horse and pony breeds.

'These ones were really clever!' James insisted. 'We had them sort of trapped down a narrow inlet. But the main mare kept them together and didn't let them panic.'

'Connemara ponies are calm,' Adam Hope agreed. 'And they have a reputation for being excellent jumpers.'

'We didn't see that,' Mandy admitted. 'But they could gallop like the wind.' She recalled the thunder of hooves as they passed by.

'I'm sure they were Connemaras,' James decided.

'And wild,' Mandy concluded.

'Well, let's ask in Molloys and find out for sure.' Emily smiled as the plate-glass shopfront came into view along the single row of terraced cottages that lined the village street. Each house-front was painted a different colour; cream, blue and pink, giving the street a holiday feel.

The name, MOLLOYS, was written in big, broad, gold letters above the door. The window to the left was stacked with packets of cornflakes and tins of baked beans; the one to the right of the red doorway with bottles of whisky and beer. A notice outside said 'Food Served All Day'.

'Chips!' Adam sighed. He held the door open and let the scent of cooking drift out. 'I'm starving!'

'You'll get fat,' Mandy's mum teased.

Inside, the shop part of Molloys was all to the

left of the door. There were shelves from floor to ceiling, stocked with sugar, dried fruit, cereals, tins of meat and vegetables. The pub part was to the right. Tall stools stood alongside the wooden and brass bar. Polished pump handles gleamed. And behind the bar, shelves were lined with glasses of all sizes waiting to be filled.

'Good evening.' A small, thin man greeted them cheerily from behind the bar. 'You must be the family that's staying at Cashel Cottages? It's your first day in Drumcashel, I hear. Well, you'll be thirsty and hungry after your boat trip out to Inishmore!'

Mandy stared at James. The barman seemed to know everything about them. His grey eyes were hidden behind deep lines and bushy eyebrows, but they had a knowing twinkle.

The few customers already leaning at the bar made room for the Hopes and James.

'You'll be liking the weather we're having,' one said to Mrs Hope. 'Sunny and fine, so it is.'

James stared back at Mandy. If this windy, misty day had been good summer weather for Drumcashel, what was bad weather likely to be?

'I'm Patrick Molloy, but you can call me Molloy like everyone else. You'll be wanting chips with everything,' the owner of the bar said without pausing for breath.

'And you're a mind-reader,' Adam Hope said quickly.

Everyone laughed.

'No one can resist the Molloys' cooking,' another customer remarked. 'Patrick's been feeding us for as long as most of us can remember, and before that it was his father and his father before him.'

'When he's not riding horses, that is.'

By now the conversation was well underway. From somewhere in a dark corner, amidst the leather seats lining the walls, an old juke-box came to life, playing an ancient pop record.

'Horses?' Mandy stepped up on to a stool at the bar and perched there eagerly. 'Do you ride?'

Molloy shrugged. 'Not any more. You're talking about me in my young days.'

'He rode his fair share of winners.' The same customer filled Mandy in by pointing to a row of faded rosettes behind the bar.

'Racing?' James joined Mandy.

'Over the hurdles,' Molloy said modestly. 'Steeplechasing was my game. It's been in the family for generations. Broke all the fingers on my right hand, three on my left. Broke my left collarbone three times, my right leg twice. Held together with steel pins from head to toe, I am.'

Mandy and James stared at the spry, slight man as he went to attend to their order for food.

'Brought up with horses, he was,' their informant told them. 'Rode them on the beach near where you're staying, long before he could even walk. Not much more than a babe in arms and he was up on a pony's back; no saddle, no bridle nor bit.'

'Really?' Mandy's mouth dropped open. Then she noticed her dad wink at her. She decided to change tack. 'Have there always been ponies on Drumcashel beach?'

'Has there always been rain on the Benmore mountains?' The young man answered with a question. He spoke slowly, in a singsong voice, as if he had all the time in the world. 'Drumcashel is practically the home of the Connemara pony. He came in with the Celts long ago when they raided these shores. They tamed him and used him for jobs around the farm and for pack work. That would be over a thousand years ago. And he's still here and will be until long after we're all pushing up the daisies!'

'And are there still herds of wild ones?' James got to the point. 'We think we saw some by the point this afternoon when the tide was coming in.'

'On Drumcashel beach?' The reply came after a long pause. 'That would be the strawberry roan's herd you spotted.'

'That's right.' Mandy nodded hard. 'She seemed to be the leader.'

'They're Sean Malone's ponies, aren't they?' another bystander chipped in.

'Oh.' James frowned. So they weren't wild, after all.

'We call them Sean's ponies because the lad spends all the days he stays here with his father looking out for them. He's known for his interest in the ponies, see. But they don't belong to him. They're wild enough, believe me.'

'That must have been the boy we saw,' James muttered to Mandy.

'His father, Gerry Malone, runs a training stable out near Lough Caher, but the two of them don't get on. Mr and Mrs Malone are divorced, and the boy is away at school most of the time. He arrived here yesterday, as a matter of fact.' The gossip flowed more quickly from the second bystander.

'The boy's about your age,' he told James and Mandy. 'A bit of a loner, but everyone round here knows him.'

Mandy and James took in every scrap of information, turning it over as the talk subsided.

'Chips coming up!' Molloy said, reappearing from the kitchen. And then it was food and the serious business of eating an enormous hot supper.

'More food!' Mandy's dad gazed bleary-eyed at the breakfast of poached eggs on toast. It was the following morning and his stomach hadn't recovered from Molloy's feast.

'Come on, wakey-wakey! We're due to set off for the races at Ballyclon in half an hour!' Emily Hope warned.

When he'd learned of the family's interest in horses, Molloy had invited them to go to the Saturday steeplechasing as his guests. He was going to pick them up in his van and drive them there.

'Uhh!' Adam groaned as he cut into his eggs.

Mandy laughed. She was curled in the window seat, looking out across the stretch of grass that led to the cliff path and the bank of fuchsia bushes to either side. The morning was clear but overcast;

probably what the locals would call great weather for the time of year. 'I thought you liked eggs on toast!' she teased.

'My eyes do, but my stomach doesn't.' Her dad struggled with his breakfast.

'Are you two ready?' Emily Hope asked James and Mandy.

'Yes. Can we go and walk on the cliff path for a few minutes?' Mandy longed to be out in the open and looking for the wild ponies again. She'd dreamed of their long, handsome faces and flowing manes; their big, dark eyes.

'Just to the fuchsia hedge, no further.' Mrs Hope wanted them nearby. 'Molloy might be early, remember.'

So they went out and ran across the grass, racing each other for a first view of the sea.

Cashel Cottages were set back a hundred metres from the cliffs, between the ruined castle on one point of land and the old church on the other. There was no road up to them; only rough tracks which the four-wheel drive had easily managed.

'They were the coastguard cottages,' Molloy had told them the night before. 'A little bit cut off from the village, but with the best view of the coast for miles around.'

Now James and Mandy saw what he meant. From the clifftop on this clear morning they could see for ever. They made out the islands scattered across the mouth of the wide bay, distant ships on the glittering horizon. And below them, at the foot of a dizzying drop, the waves crashed against the shore on to the smooth white sands.

'See anything?' James asked. He knew Mandy well enough to realise that she'd come looking for ponies.

She shook her head, searching for a way through the tall flowering hedge for a better view of the beaches. 'Maybe they only go down there in the afternoons.'

But she spoke too soon. As they peered over the cliff, she heard movement on the clifftop near the castle and turned to look. There, about two hundred metres away, on the narrow point of land, a herd of ponies had gathered.

James saw them at the same time as Mandy. 'It's the same ones!' he whispered.

The ponies milled quietly in the shelter of a ruined wall. Some lowered their heads to graze. A tiny foal suckled from a dun mare.

'There's the strawberry roan.' In her mind Mandy chose a name for the beautiful pony.

'Rosie!' she murmured. 'And her foal is Connie, after Connemara!'

'They're coming this way!' James stepped behind the hedge to hide. 'Duck down, Mandy. We might get a really close view!'

Mandy crouched low as Rosie trotted in a circle round the herd, then led them away from the point across the stretch of open grassland towards the hedge. She and James were downwind and well-hidden. But they could see the wild ponies through gaps in the hedge and, sure enough, they came in twos and threes, following the roan leader along a track worn into the grass.

'Where are they going? They're heading for the edge of the cliff!' James whispered, almost jumping up to stop them.

'No; there's a path!' Mandy held his arm. She saw Rosie pick out a way down a part of the cliff that dropped down gradually from one ledge to another, instead of in one sheer stretch. It must be the ponies' way down to the smooth sands where they could gallop free. 'She knows what she's doing!'

The ponies passed less than fifty metres from where they hid. Their hooves caught on loose stones and sent them sliding and clattering down

the rocks. The lead mare paused to wait, letting her foal shelter against her flank on the side closest to James and Mandy.

'Look!' Mandy held on to James's sleeve and pointed with her other hand. She could hardly believe what she saw; something they'd missed on the beach the day before, when the whole herd had kept their distance.

James stared at the chestnut foal. 'What's she got round her head?' he gasped.

Mandy looked more closely to make sure she wasn't mistaken. She made out a rough halter made of rope, knotted and tied across the foal's nose and cheeks. 'Someone's put a headcollar on her!' she whispered. 'But she must have been a lot smaller when they did it. It's much too small for her now!'

The foal waited patiently at her mother's side. She was close enough for them to see the frayed rope and the ugly knots, the places on her cheeks and nose where the headcollar had rubbed and cut into the dark brown coat.

'Who would do that?' James shifted his position. The mare lifted her head and flicked her ears.

'Someone who wanted to capture her, I expect.' Mandy frowned. Seeing the cruel rope on the wild pony made her frightened and angry. She felt like rushing to cut the rope and save the foal from its painful pressure.

'No!' It was James's turn to hold on to her. 'We could scare her!' He pointed to the steep drop over the cliff. The lead mare was already restless, waiting for the rest of the herd to catch up before she could move on. Perhaps she sensed James and Mandy hiding behind the bank.

'But we can't just leave her to suffer!' Mandy hissed.

'We have to!' James insisted. If the herd took flight on that dangerous, steep track, there would be a disaster. 'What's the worst that could happen if the collar stays on?'

Mandy dug her fingernails into her palms and watched in horror as Rosie moved on at last. She saw Connie shake her head as if the rope bothered her, then follow shakily.

'Come on, Mandy. What do you think would happen to the foal?' James wanted to know.

She sighed. Connie vanished out of sight, followed by the suckling mare and her tiny foal. 'I don't know for sure. We'll have to check with Mum and Dad. But I suppose as she grows the headcollar would cut deeper and deeper into her flesh,' she said in a shaky voice. 'The wound would become open and raw.'

'Would it get infected?'

Mandy nodded. She didn't say any more because she wasn't completely sure. But she and James both realised what this might mean. Left untreated, an infected wound could poison Connie's whole system. Sooner or later, if the headcollar wasn't removed, the little brown foal could die.

Three

Molloy's rusty white van came rattling down the track to Cashel Cottages. He was calling, as planned, to take the visitors to Ballyclon races.

As the ex-jockey jumped out and banged on the door, Mandy and James ran back from the edge of the cliff. They'd come to a decision.

'Mum, Dad, is it OK if James and I stay here?' Mandy asked breathlessly, after they'd greeted Molloy. She knew that her parents must stick by their promise to go with Molloy. She would tell them about the problem with the foal later, but

for now she and James would see what they could
do to help.

'What? Not come to the races?' Emily Hope
raised her eyebrows.

'That must be a first!' agreed Adam, with a grin.
'Mandy and James turning down the chance to
get close to a bunch of beautiful, highly-trained,
superbly fit animals!'

'We just saw the wild ponies again!' James
explained. 'They're down on the beach, right now.'

Molloy nodded. 'That'll be right. Every morning, and again in the afternoon, Sean Malone's
herd takes that cliff path down to the sea. There's
drinking water down there, see.'

'Where?' James was puzzled. How could ponies
drink the salt seawater?

'There's a stream that runs down to meet the
sea in Kilmore Cove. It gathers in a pool called
Blackrock. That's where the ponies are heading
for, you can be sure.'

'Thanks,' Mandy said. She turned to her mum
and dad. 'We won't go any further than Kilmore
Cove,' she promised.

'No swimming without supervision,' Mrs Hope
instructed, laying out the conditions for letting
them stay.

'No way!' Mandy shivered and huddled her arms across her chest.

'No risky rock-climbing.'

'We'll use the path,' James agreed.

'I'm still not sure.' Emily glanced at Adam. 'We'll be away for most of the day. It seems an awful long time to leave you to your own devices.'

'Why not let the young ones stay here for an hour or so, if that's what they want to do?' Molloy suggested. 'Then they can come and join us at Ballyclon. Your neighbour, Tom O'Rourke, can bring them along later.'

Mandy seized on the idea. 'Great!'

'I didn't know we had any neighbours,' Adam Hope said, looking round at the great open space of sea and sky.

'Tom lives at the farm beyond the church on the point,' Molloy explained. 'He's a great man for the horses. And I know for a fact that he'll be coming along to the races later this morning. We can call in at his house as we pass by and ask him to give these two a lift!'

And so it was arranged. Mandy and James would be able to investigate the wild herd, and Adam and Emily Hope's minds would be set at rest.

tame any wild ponies!' Adam
...ng out of Molloy's window with one
...ction.

...y smiled. 'OK!' she called after him.
...emember,' he shouted, 'they can give you a
hefty kick with those hooves!'

'What shall we take with us?' Mandy asked James.

They were hunting in the small, dark outhouse attached to Cashel Cottages.

'If we're going to try and help the foal now we'll need to catch her first,' James replied. 'So we need to find some rope to make lassoes with.' Then he frowned. 'But remember what your dad said Mandy. We'll have to be careful. Those ponies are wild – they could be dangerous if we upset them.'

Mandy nodded her head. 'I know, James,' she replied. 'But we won't do anything silly. OK?' As she reassured him, Mandy moved towards the outhouse door. 'We'll need a knife to cut the headcollar off,' she said. 'I'll bring my penknife.' She went back to the cottage to fetch it.

When Mandy returned, James was emerging into the daylight with two coils of rope. 'Here!' he said. 'Just what we were looking for.'

Mandy took one from him. They made rough

nooses with slipknots in the lengths of rope.

'Right, I've got the penknife,' Mandy confirmed. 'Let's go!'

They set off eagerly towards the cliff path.

'With the wind coming off the sea we should be able to work our way near to the herd without them getting scent of us and taking flight,' Mandy said as they ran. 'Then, if we can get a rope round Connie's neck, it should only take a couple of seconds to cut through the headcollar.'

'But it all depends on us getting close enough,' James replied.

They reached the cliff and looked down at the beach. Breathing hard, steadying themselves as they gazed down the steep drop, they picked out the telltale trail of hoofprints across the sand. Though they couldn't see the herd, the evidence indicated that the ponies had headed as usual for the tucked-away corner of Kilmore Cove.

'This is the only way up and down,' James confirmed, pointing to the narrow, stony track, then letting his gaze sweep along the cliffs that fringed the bay. His face set in a frown as he fixed his sights on the tall stone cross that stood in the church grounds at the very edge of the cliff.

Quickly Mandy looked that way too. 'Sean

Malone,' she murmured, recognising the dark hair and slight figure of the boy that Molloy had told them about. She felt uncomfortable at being watched again. 'It could have been Sean Malone who fitted that headcollar to Connie in the first place.'

Equally ill at ease, James jumped to a conclusion. 'He probably wanted to catch her when he was here during the spring holidays so he could take her home to his father's training stables!'

'Ignore him,' Mandy said. 'Come on, let's go.'

They picked their way silently down, catching their breath whenever their feet dislodged a stone and sent it tumbling down the rocky slope.

Mandy clung to a tree root for safety, then steadied herself before she picked her way on. They were still ten metres above the sands, looking anxiously for the herd. The wind from the sea tore at her clothes and tugged at her hair, the heavy rope dragged at her shoulder.

'You think Sean wanted to break Connie in and use her as a trekking pony at the school?' Mandy considered the theory, then shrugged. 'I suppose he could have put the headcollar on last time he was home. But we don't know that, do we?'

'Why else would he watch the herd all the time?' James held on to his idea. 'He's probably waiting until he sees that Connie is separated from Rosie, then he can move in and try again. Only Connie sticks close to her mother all the time, so Sean never gets the chance!'

'Hmm.' Mandy saw that this gave her and James a problem too. 'Come to that, how are *we* going to corner Connie without Rosie trying to protect her?'

She'd reached the beach and turned to wait. Way above, at the foot of the stone cross, the boy still watched their progress.

'We'll try and creep up on them while they're still in the cove,' James suggested. 'Then, when Rosie does her thing of rounding the others up and keeping them in order, that's when we seize our chance with Connie, OK?'

Mandy nodded. She suspected that James sounded more confident than he felt.

She followed him, testing the direction of the wind to make sure that they didn't stray upwind of the ponies.

After a few minutes' trek across the sand, skirting the bottom of the towering cliffs and making for the inlet where they knew the ponies would be drinking, they came to the mouth of the narrow cove.

James paused for breath at last. He pressed back against the rough surface of the rock, ready to peer around the final corner.

Mandy stayed hidden. She listened hard, able to make out a soft trickle of running water and the track of a clear stream as it cut through the soft sand towards the sea. 'Are they there?' she whispered to James.

'I can see a couple. The rest must be inside the cave. Take a look.' He gave up his position to Mandy.

She craned her head round the rock and gave a little gasp as she realised how close the straggler ponies were; perhaps only twenty to thirty metres from where she and James were hidden. She recognised the badly-behaved young grey stallion from the previous day, then spotted the black and white piebald that had taken the kick in the flank. Today they lowered their heads and drank peaceably from the same stream.

Then the other ponies emerged from the dark cave, stepping into the daylight with a toss of the head or a quick kick of the heels. Mandy gestured to James to come and see.

'They must be getting ready to leave!' James said with a touch of panic in his voice. He took the coil of rope from his shoulder and stood poised to throw it.

'Here come Rosie and Connie.' Mandy saw that the mare and her foal were the last to leave the cave. Now Rosie was sniffing the air with her flaring nostrils, her ears flicking this way and that.

'Has she spotted us?' James drew back quickly and pressed against the rock.

Mandy kept her nerve and stayed where she was. 'Maybe. But it's a dead-end; they have to come this way in any case. She's rounding them all up. Stand by, James!'

Rosie trotted to the front of the group, nudging the young ones with her nose, kicking up the sand with her high-stepping trot. As always, little Connie stuck close to her heels.

Mandy stepped back out of sight and got her rope ready. Even if the first throw failed, it might succeed in splitting Connie off from her mother. That would give them the chance to trap the smaller, weaker foal, move in on her and get to work on the tight collar that Mandy could see now. The home-made headcollar cut deep into Connie's chin groove and nose, and chafed at the

spot behind her ears where it looped over her head.

They heard the thud of the ponies' hooves as the herd kicked into action. They drummed across the wet sand, splashed in the shallow stream. They were almost at the mouth of the cove.

'Now!' Mandy whispered.

She and James stepped out, whirling the long ropes above their heads. Rosie was two or three strides away. She saw them and reared up, turning aside and steering the herd against the opposite wall of rock. Caught by surprise, Connie dug in her heels and stopped.

Mandy took one pace towards the startled foal. She aimed the noose and flung the rope through the air. It snaked towards Connie but fell far short.

James swung his rope above his head. He threw. The second noose fell uselessly to the ground.

Then Rosie turned back to face them. She came between them and her foal, her nostrils flared wide as she reared up and pawed the air. They glimpsed her dark-brown underbelly.

Thud! Her front hooves landed. She stood facing them, guarding her foal, warning them off. Connie cowered in her shadow, showing the whites of her eyes, tottering backwards towards the far cliff.

Mandy pulled her rope back towards her and stooped to gather it. James let his lie where it was. 'There's no point,' he whispered, unable to take his eyes off the angry mare. 'She'll never let us near!'

'If only she could understand that we're trying to help!' But Mandy knew James was right. Every inch of flesh on Rosie's strong body quivered with rage. She reared again and flashed her hooves through the air. Mandy remembered her father's words of warning.

'She thinks we're the enemy.' James stepped back. He watched the whole herd take refuge behind Rosie, waiting for the order to move out on to the open beach.

'We're not. We're your friends!' Mandy cried out loud.

Her words were wasted. They flew off into the wind as Rosie reared again and whirled round, gathering Connie and leading the herd away.

The ponies trampled James's rope into the sand as they fled. The foal still wore her cruel head-collar.

'If only we could talk to them.' Mandy sighed.

The ponies were free of the cove, splashing through the shallow white waves on the shore. 'If only they understood!'

Normally, the brightly-coloured silks of the jockeys' shirts, the buzz of the crowd and the sight of well-groomed horses parading in the paddock would have thrilled Mandy and brought her to the edge of her seat in the grandstand.

Today was different. She sat quietly, taking hardly any interest in the starters in the Ballyclon Gold Cup.

'Not feeling too good?' Adam Hope leaned across.

'No, I'm fine, Dad . . . thanks.'

Their neighbour, Tom O'Rourke, had driven Mandy and James to the races as planned. He was a tall, heavily-built man who didn't speak much, but that had been fine by them. They hadn't felt like talking either, after the failure of their plan in Kilmore Cove.

'Want to tell me about it?' her dad said gently, as the jockeys mounted their horses and the people in the crowd laid their final flurry of bets.

Mandy glanced at his friendly, kind face, his warm, brown eyes. Then the whole story of

Connie and the headcollar poured out.

'We wanted Rosie to trust us!' she whispered. 'But she wouldn't.'

'This is a wild creature we're talking about.' Adam Hope had listened to her thoughtfully. 'They're either going to fight you or take off, depending on whether they're "fight" animals like the big cats and wild dogs, or "flight" animals like deer and horses. No way was that mare going to stick around and let you put a rope round her foal's neck.'

Mandy sighed. 'I suppose I knew that, really. But Connie's in pain. She must be suffering, Dad!'

'And you felt you had to do something?'

She nodded. By now the horses and their riders had passed out on to the racetrack and were heading for the starting stalls. 'James thinks that Sean Malone wanted to catch the foal and tame her,' she explained. 'That's how she came to be wearing the headcollar in the first place.'

'But she escaped?' Adam Hope considered this and leaned the other way to talk to Molloy about it. 'Would people round here try to capture the wild Connemaras?' he asked.

The shopkeeper narrowed his eyes and kept his gaze fixed on the start of the race. 'No, not at all,' he replied. 'It's against the law for a start.'

'And? . . . What else?' Mandy prompted. Molloy seemed sure that James's theory was wrong.

Down on the track, the starter raised his arm. The horses were ready for the off.

'Secondly, if anyone round here were to lay a hand on the wild ponies, the rest of us wouldn't just stand by and let it happen, let me tell you.' Molloy grunted as the race began. The doors of the stalls lifted and the horses surged forward along the smooth green track.

'It's true we don't interfere with the Connemaras.' The shopkeeper went on to describe the local people's point of view. 'We like to let them keep their distance. But it doesn't mean we don't care.'

'So who else might be interested in capturing them?' Adam Hope persisted.

'That would be an outsider you're talking about,' Molloy told them. 'Someone from across the water. They sometimes come after the ponies with their vans and their trailers. They load them up and take them back where they came from to sell to the highest bidder, no questions asked.'

'Abroad?' Mandy's dad frowned. He spoke above the shouts of the crowd as the horses rounded the first bend. 'Is this an illegal trade you're talking about?'

Molloy nodded and jumped to his feet. 'Come on, Playboy!' His favourite horse took the next bend ahead of the field. 'That's right,' he told them. 'I hear there's good money in taking the ponies back to France or England. Come on, Playboy, you can do it!' He raised his arms and yelled.

Mandy sagged in her seat. The first horse had passed the winning-post and the crowd went wild. But Molloy's version of what must have nearly happened to Connie sent a shiver through her.

'This is worse than Sean Malone,' she told herself. 'This could be organised, international horse-stealing we're dealing with!'

Four

'So no one can get near this foal?' Emily Hope asked when she heard of Connie's predicament.

The day at the races was over, and Molloy was dropping them off at Cashel Cottages. He'd shaken his head at Mandy's description of the headcollar, and now he gave his opinion: 'The sooner nature takes its course the better.'

'What do you mean?' James asked.

'Well, if there's nothing we can do to help the poor creature, we just have to hope that she's soon put out of her misery.' He understood that the headcollar would grow so tight that it would eventually cut through the flesh of the face. 'I never like to see an animal suffer,' he concluded quietly.

So they stood outside their low, whitewashed cottage by the four-wheel drive, watching Molloy drive off.

'We did try,' James sighed. He stared out at the red sun sinking towards the watery horizon.

'But not hard enough.' Mandy couldn't let it drop. 'Isn't there something else we could do?' she pleaded.

Her mother thought long and hard before she came up with an idea. 'Now, you might not like what I'm about to suggest,' she warned James and Mandy. 'But listen and consider it before you say anything.'

They nodded and looked earnestly at her.

'It's what Adam and I might use as a last resort when we're dealing with a large farm animal at home,' Mrs Hope went on. 'From the outside it might seem cruel, but it's a very effective way of going about treating horses and cattle if the patient isn't likely to cooperate.' She glanced at Adam Hope for support.

'You mean Immobilon?' he said quietly.

'Yes. It's a very strong drug,' she told a worried

Mandy and James. 'We use it as a tranquilliser. It knocks an animal unconscious within seconds. Then we treat the patient and afterwards inject an antidote. The animal recovers and is up on its feet before it realises what's happened.'

Mandy swallowed hard. 'Is the drug dangerous?'

Emily paused, then nodded. 'Actually, it's so strong that it would be fatal to a human being. So, yes, it's very dangerous. But we control the dosage for the animals we treat. That means we measure the exact amount we need to tranquillise the patient. With the little foal you're talking about it would probably be a one millilitre dose.'

'Wait!' James interrupted. 'This Immobilon may work like you say it does, but it still doesn't solve the problem of getting near enough to Connie to inject her with it in the first place. How do you get over that one?'

'Ah!' Adam Hope had been expecting the question. 'That's the risky bit. We can't inject the patient with a syringe in a case like this. Instead, we use a dart.'

'And a gun?' Mandy asked quietly. She pictured the scene, remembering the time when she'd been in Africa and a dart gun had been used to immobilise a wounded elephant.

'We use a special rifle. The dart is pushed down the barrel with a coloured ribbon-marker attached. We aim and fire the dart into muscle on the animal's flank. Like I said, the drug works in seconds.'

'But what if you don't aim well?' James broke in again. 'Or what if the animal moves suddenly?'

'That's part of the risk,' Mandy's mum admitted. 'Like I said, I see the method as a last resort. But if the foal is likely to die anyway of an infected wound, I don't really see the alternative.'

'But it seems so cruel!' Mandy closed her eyes and tried not to think about the dart piercing Connie's side. The foal would stagger and fall with the rest of the herd looking on. She would lie unconscious and Rosie would think she was dead.

'What do you want us to do?' Emily Hope waited for them to consider the problem from all angles. 'If you like, we could try what I've suggested. We've got the equipment with us in the back of the four-wheel drive. But if you can't face it, we won't do it.'

'It's too late today, anyway,' James pointed out. 'The herd will have been to drink in the cove and gone again.'

'But there's always tomorrow.' As the shadows

lengthened and the wind grew chilly, Adam Hope turned the key in the cottage door, ready to go inside.

Mandy gazed at the sunset. The sun seemed to meet the sea and spill liquid gold on to the water. 'They'll come back after breakfast,' she whispered. 'Molloy says they always do.'

'Does that mean we should go ahead?' her mum asked.

Mandy turned to James. Through a deep frown he gave a faint blink and a nod.

'Yes.' She walked away, across the grass to the bank of bright pink fuchsias, to watch the sun sink into the sea.

The next day dawned grey and misty.

'This is what Ireland is famous for; wet mist creeping across the peat-bogs. A land of bare purple mountains, rocky streams, deserted cottages . . .' Adam Hope tried to lighten the mood over breakfast. 'At least, that's what it said in my tourist brochure!'

Mandy managed a strained smile. She'd hardly slept for thinking about what they were about to do.

'What if firing the tranquilliser dart scares the

others off?' was the first thing she'd said to her mum. 'Rosie might desert Connie and never come back!'

'Mandy!' Emily Hope squeezed her shoulder. 'Don't torture yourself. That's a very unlikely possibility, you know!'

'But, what if—?'

'Listen, the mare is much more likely to keep a safe distance while we move in and treat the foal's wounds. It wouldn't be at all natural for her to desert her offspring.'

'Perhaps you and James had better stay here while your mum and I go down to the beach,' Adam Hope suggested now. 'That way, you won't have to go through all the suspense of watching.'

'Oh no!' James jumped up from the table. 'I'm ready. I want to come.'

'Me too.' Mandy knew she had to face it. This is what happened if you were a vet; you took risks, made judgements and carried them through into action. If the tranquilliser dart was the only way to save Connie's life, then they all had to be part of it.

So they set off together. Emily Hope took her bag from the back of the four-wheel drive. Adam Hope carried the rifle.

'This way.' James led them to the steep track and showed them the way down. 'Be careful of this next bit,' he warned at a stretch of the track that was especially slippery.

'It's OK, there's no need to rush.' Mandy brought up the rear of the party. She stopped to study the smooth, unmarked beach. 'The herd hasn't come down to drink yet.'

'That means we can find a good position to hide before they get there.' Emily Hope thought ahead as she scrambled down, bag in hand. 'We should choose a spot with a good view of the ponies as they come into the cove.'

'Inside the cave,' James suggested. 'They won't be able to see us or smell us if we're hiding in there.'

'I hope it's not too misty for us to see them properly.' Mandy imagined another hitch. 'There's more than one foal in the herd. We have to be sure we get Connie and not one of the others!'

'Don't worry. I'll wait until you're absolutely sure,' Emily Hope promised. Mandy's mum had decided to be the one who fired the dart gun.

They reached the beach and headed for Kilmore Cove, past a short row of upturned curraghs.

'I'd rather be out in one of those than doing this, and that's saying something!' Mandy said grimly.

Adam Hope put an arm round her shoulder and walked with her. 'It'll soon be over,' he assured her. 'Trust me. We'll cut through the headcollar that's causing the problem, give the little foal a shot of antibiotics, inject the antidote, then she'll be up on her feet and away!'

Taking a deep breath, Mandy led the way into the cave. 'Mind you don't step in the stream!' she called. The fresh water of Blackrock Pool trickled through a fissure in the rocks and collected in a shallow pool at the mouth of the cave. From there, it gradually drained into another stream that fed into the sea. The cave dripped and echoed.

James flashed a torch around the high, arched roof. Water glistened on every surface, but he spotted a fairly dry ledge where they could all wait until the wild ponies turned up to drink.

'You go on ahead.' Emily Hope agreed that it would be a good hiding-place. 'I'll fix the dart into the gun before I climb up.'

So Mandy, James and Adam Hope took up their position.

'It's a good job the tide's out,' Mandy's dad said

as he climbed on to the rough ledge. He pointed to clumps of dark seaweed stranded by the last high tide. 'The water obviously covers the whole beach and comes up as far as the ledge.'

Mandy pictured the slap and crash of giant waves as they smashed through the cave entrance and swirled against the walls. She shuddered and crouched down to wait. 'Hurry up, Mum!' she urged.

'Coming!' Emily Hope slid the dart into place, then she joined them on the ledge. 'I think I heard movement out on the beach,' she told them, squatting closest to the entrance where she could get the best view.

But she'd obviously been mistaken about the sounds. The wait went on for fifteen minutes, stretching to half an hour. Their legs grew cramped, their clothes cold and wet from the dripping roof.

Then they heard it; the unmistakable sound of hooves, drawing nearer.

Mandy crouched beside her mother. She saw her raise the rifle to shoulder level. In the entrance to the cave, the first pony appeared.

With the daylight behind the animal, they could only make out the silhouette. But Mandy recognised the raised head, the stamping hoof, of the lead mare. As usual, Rosie was the first to venture into the dark cave. And close at her heels came Connie.

Mandy tugged sharply at her mother's jacket. 'That's her!' she whispered.

Rosie's head jerked quickly back. She'd heard Mandy's voice.

Emily Hope aimed the tranquilliser gun at Connie. She began to squeeze the trigger.

Then time seemed to stand still.

A human figure stepped across the entrance, arms raised, voice shouting. 'Get out of here!' he yelled at the ponies. 'Go on, run!'

Mrs Hope's aim shook. She lowered the gun.

'What the . . . ?' Adam Hope leaped down from the ledge and ran towards the noisy intruder. 'Do you want to get yourself killed?'

In the confusion, Rosie reared up. She squealed with fright and whirled round, coming between Mandy's mum and her foal.

'It's no good.' Emily Hope wouldn't risk firing the dart under these conditions. She leaned the gun against the rock and put on the safety catch. Today wasn't the day for carrying out the plan to save the foal.

Mandy swayed this way and that, trying to see what was going on. Her dad was still running to stop the figure from spooking the ponies. But it was too late. The intruder whirled his arms and yelled. Rosie steered Connie out on to the safety of the open sands.

'You know who that is, don't you?' she cried to James, jumping on to the wet sand beneath their ledge.

'Sean Malone!'

Who else? 'Don't you realise what you've just

done?' Mandy cried. Angrily she ran to confront the boy.

The ponies scattered across the bay, manes streaming. Soon the mist would swallow them and only the sound of their hooves drumming on the sand would show where they were heading.

'Yes.' The thin, dark-haired boy who'd watched them from a distance now stood sullenly in Mandy's way. His grey eyes flashed, his wide mouth scowled. 'I've stopped you from shooting the ponies.'

'No!' she yelled. How could he be so stupid?

'I saw you come in here with the gun.' He wouldn't back down. He stared angrily, his short, straight hair ruffled by the wind, his dark eyebrows knotted in a frown.

'That wasn't real ammunition!' Mandy gasped with frustration. 'We weren't going to shoot the foal with bullets!'

Sean Malone turned away scornfully. He wouldn't even stop to listen to her weird explanation.

'It's a tranquilliser dart!' She ran after him. 'We were trying to knock the foal out so we could treat the wounds on her face, that's all!'

The boy stopped dead. He let the wind blow against his T-shirt and bare arms as Mandy's words sank in.

She ran to confront him face to face. 'Now do you see? My mum and dad are vets. Without their help, Connie will die!'

Five

'It sounds like you and young Sean Malone got your wires crossed,' Molloy said as he served coffee and biscuits to the visitors next morning.

Mandy stroked a long-haired white cat with yellow eyes that sat by the iron stove behind the bar. 'Sean didn't know that Mum and Dad were vets,' she explained. They'd told their sympathetic new friend all about the events on the beach the day before. 'That's why he stepped in and spooked the ponies like he did.'

'And I was wrong to think he was the one who'd

tried to catch Connie in the first place,' James admitted.

When Molloy smiled, his eyes vanished behind deep wrinkles. 'We all make mistakes. If you're big enough to admit them, that's the main thing.'

'It turns out Sean wouldn't dream of going near the wild ponies,' Mandy went on. The white cat purred as she tickled her chin. 'That was part of the problem really; he'd never gone near enough to the herd to spot the headcollar on Connie, so he didn't know about her injury. He just watches them from the point of land by the church.'

'Ah, but you should see him when he does go near a horse. He has a way with them; a gift,' the shopkeeper informed them. 'I've seen him approach a young unbroken colt; within thirty minutes he can have that horse eating out of his hand!'

Mandy leaned across the bar. 'Really?'

Molloy nodded. 'You'd swear he was actually talking to the horse the way he gains its trust and gets in close.'

'That sounds like a great talent to have,' James said. He was intrigued by this new picture of Sean Malone. When Mandy and the hostile boy had stood face to face in Kilmore Cove, shouting about poor Connie, James had realised that Sean *did* care about the ponies after all. But he'd had no inkling of this reputation for "talking" to them.

'You're not wrong there,' Molloy replied. 'But then, every Irishman considers himself an expert on the horses. Did you know, in this country we have a race meeting on two hundred and fifty days of each year!'

'I've noticed a lot of racecourses,' James said.

'And riding-schools,' Mandy added.

'And of course, all the training stables and gallops for the racehorses,' Emily Hope added. 'I suppose that's the sort of place that Sean's father runs?'

'Over at Lough Caher,' Molloy agreed. He poured a saucer of milk for the cat and handed it to Mandy. 'Put the dish where Misty can see it,' he told her. 'She's stone-deaf, so she won't hear you call.'

Mandy placed the saucer by the stove and watched the cat sniff at it. She gave Misty an extra stroke, admiring how the deaf cat coped in her silent world. The cat lowered her head and lapped eagerly with her pink tongue.

'Of course, in a country full of experts, you have as many different opinions about the horses as there are people to express them,' said Molloy, leaning across the bar. With no other customers and time to kill, he was enjoying the chat. 'Take Sean Malone and his father, Gerry.'

'Ah yes; we heard that they didn't get on.' Emily Hope remembered hearing on their first visit to Molloys that Sean's parents were separated and Sean away at school. She sat with her elbows on the bar, hair loose over her shoulders, dressed in her holiday clothes of T-shirt and shorts.

'Gerry's one of the old school as far as training horses is concerned,' Molloy explained. 'With Gerry and a horse it's always a question of who's the boss, whereas the young lad, he's different.'

'How, different?'

Molloy cocked his head sideways. 'The way I see it, Sean doesn't try to bully a horse. He watches what they do, and he seems to tune in to that.'

'You mean, he *behaves* like a horse?' Mandy was puzzled but fascinated.

'Not exactly. I've studied what it is he does with a horse that's been playing up badly when I've been over at Lough Caher. But, hard as I try, I can never pin it down.'

'Does he actually *say* anything to the horse?' James asked.

'No. It's not talking, it's more like a silent language. You'd have to ask him.' Molloy said this with a wink at Adam and Emily Hope.

'Couldn't you just describe it to us?' Mandy was nervous about meeting up with Sean Malone again, after what had happened yesterday. She'd shouted at him to stop spooking the ponies and he'd yelled back until they'd both made themselves hoarse. She'd blamed him for not letting them help Connie. In the end, he'd run off along the beach.

'You have to see for yourselves.' The ex-jockey shrugged. 'It's a terrible pity to pass up the chance of getting to know Sean better,' he told them. 'If you could work out his secret, sure you could bottle it and make yourselves a fortune!'

'Thanks for the lift,' Mandy said to her dad.

Adam Hope was dropping them off at Lough Caher Training Yard later that day. The sign over the gate was new and smart, the fields to either side of the wide drive were smooth and lush.

'If you've come to learn the horse gift from Sean Malone, let me give you a word of warning,' Mandy's dad said. 'Just remember that Molloy might be exaggerating a teeny bit!' He didn't want them to have false hopes about the boy's way with horses.

'OK. Thanks.' For a second, Mandy's hopes sank. She frowned at James but then squared her shoulders. 'Anyway, let's wait and see.'

'You're sure you don't want me to wait for you?' Mandy's dad checked again.

'No thanks.' She read the small lettering on the sign under the name of the yard: GERALD MALONE, RACEHORSE TRAINER. BOARDING FACILITIES AVAILABLE.

'What if Sean doesn't want to see you two?' Mr Hope asked. 'It's a long walk back to Drumcashel.'

'We'll manage, thanks,' James told him.

'Hmm. Well, it looks a pretty posh place.' Mr Hope leaned out of the car window and took in the half-dozen thoroughbred horses grazing in the fields. 'You'd better be on your best behaviour.'

'We will!' James called back, as he and Mandy set off up the drive.

'Well, we'll try!' she smiled, marching on. Places like Lough Caher Training Yard set her teeth on edge. They were too neat and tidy; the fences were painted too white, the hedges clipped too short. Even the horses were too groomed and plaited, rugged and clipped, to look real.

At the end of the drive they came to a gated yard. Beyond the gate was a square of low, stone-built stable buildings. Each stable had a bright white door with black hinges. The yard was swept perfectly clean.

'Yes?' A man came out of an ivy-covered office building to one side of the square. He was tall, slim and good-looking, dressed in a pale blue cotton shirt and jeans.

'Mr Malone?' Mandy recognised Sean's dark hair and grey eyes in the man's appearance.

He nodded. 'We don't do riding lessons here. This is a training yard for racehorses,' he said curtly, eyeing them up and down. He obviously dismissed Mandy and James in their summer shorts and trainers as time-wasting tourists.

'We know,' James said quietly.

'And we don't do pony-trekking either. If it's that sort of thing you're after, look for the riding-school in Drumcashel.' Gerry Malone turned on his heel, as good as telling them to clear off.

'We've come to see Sean,' Mandy said, before he could disappear into the office.

The man paused in the doorway. 'You know my son?' he asked sharply.

'We met him yesterday.' James was careful not

to say how or where. 'Mr Molloy told us this was where he lived.'

The boss of the yard lost interest. 'Molloy's an old gossip. He should mind his own business. But since you're here, you'll find Sean mucking out in the stables opposite,' he told them. 'You can talk to him, but don't stop him from working. We're a man short today, so Sean is covering for him.'

As the door swung closed, Mandy and James went to look in the empty stables. They glimpsed a tack-room with rows of saddle and bridle racks, and grooming kits neatly laid out on tables. The dark-brown leather saddles gleamed, the silver bits and bridles glittered.

Then they came to the first row of stables. Mandy and James glanced inside the half-open doors one by one, noticing the freshly filled mangers and buckets, the new beds of straw on the floor. The work had been done, but there was no sign of Sean.

'Maybe he's out with one of the horses,' James suggested, almost ready to give up. Even if they found the boy, there was no guarantee that he would want to make friends.

Mandy peered down a path that led down the side of a stable block towards a large stone barn.

The doors of the barn were open and she made out a covered arena with raked seats to one side and an exercise area for training horses. 'How about in there?' she said quietly, listening to the sound of hooves drumming round the arena.

They followed the sound. Standing at the door of the barn, they found Sean at last.

He stood in the centre of the training ring, silently watching a horse trot round it. The horse was a bay mare with long legs and a graceful neck. She wore a headcollar, but no bridle or bit, and she ran free. Her head was up and her ears were pricked towards Sean in the middle of the ring.

Sean had his eyes fixed on the mare, but he must have spotted Mandy and James as they came into the barn. 'Stay over there until I've finished,' he said in a calm voice. He didn't seem surprised or upset to see them.

'What are you doing?' James climbed some wooden steps to a row of benches and looked down on the arena. Mandy stayed at ground level, leaning on the low fence.

'Working with the horse.' Sean kept his gaze steadily on the mare. 'We have to get rid of some faults.'

Mandy frowned. What did Sean mean,

'working'? Where was the long rope called a lunge rein needed to keep the horse in check? 'What's wrong with her?' she asked.

'She's started to buck her riders. She's a young horse and it's a bad habit.' Sean still concentrated on the mare. Whenever she seemed to want to stop trotting round the outside edge of the ring, he would square up to her and wave his arms. This sent her off at a canter, as far away from him as possible.

'So you're lunging her without a rope?' Mandy got the idea.

'Yep.' He stared at the horse's head, keeping square on to her as she cantered. 'I'm saying, "Keep your distance. I don't want you to come near." I'm waiting for her to ask me to come in from the fence again.'

'How can she do that?' James sat on the edge of his seat. The mare certainly seemed to be keeping her distance, as Sean wanted.

'She'll give me some signals that she wants to "talk".' Slowly Sean let his own gaze drift from the mare's head, down her neck to a spot on her powerful shoulders. Meanwhile, the horse's ears flicked towards him and she ducked her head. 'See that?' Sean asked, his own gaze locked on to her shoulder now. 'That means, "OK, I'm listening to you! What do you want me to do?" '

The bay mare slowed down to a trot, waiting for a response from the boy.

'But I'm only going to talk when I'm ready,' Sean explained. He was so caught up in his training method that he seemed to have forgotten the quarrel of the day before. He squared up to the mare again and sent her cantering wide. He made her work until her head went down to within a few centimetres of the ground, then he let her slow to a trot and come off the fence.

'See that!' Sean breathed. There was warm satisfaction in his voice. His thin face was flushed and eager. 'This time she really wants to come back in and talk, and this time I'm ready to let her.' He took his eyes off the tired horse, going right up to her now and reaching out to rub her between the eyes.

They stood only metres from where Mandy watched. She saw Sean turn slowly away from the problem horse. The mare followed as if attached by a lead. He turned another way. She followed again.

'She trusts me,' he told them. 'Because I know how she thinks. She doesn't want to be out there

cantering round the ring for ever. She wants me to be nice to her.' Smoothly he took hold of the mare's headcollar and stroked her again, being careful not to make eye contact. 'Some people use force to get a horse to do as they're told, but I don't believe in that.'

'What now?' Mandy asked. Though she agreed with the no-force theory, she wondered deep down whether the method Sean had just demonstrated could be some sort of fluke.

'That's enough for now. Next time we work, I'll saddle her up and go through the same thing all over again; sending her out to the rim of the paddock, making her keep her distance until she's ready to do a deal with me.'

'Then will you put the bridle on?' Mandy saw that it was a patient, slow process to cure the mare of her bad habit of bucking. For now, she followed Sean as he led the horse out of the arena.

'When she's happy to let me,' Sean replied.

'How long will it take?' James came down from his bench and joined them.

'Maybe two more sessions . . .' Sean rewarded the mare with more rubs. 'After that, she should be cured.'

Mandy nodded thoughtfully. 'And you're sure that wasn't a coincidence we just saw?' She spoke her doubts and felt Sean stiffen up.

'You sound like my dad!' He cast a defiant look at the office building. 'I show him once and he says it's a fluke. I show him twice, three times, and according to him, it's still not really happening. He says I was just lucky. I haven't actually shown him a new way to train a horse!'

Mandy heard the anger in his voice and decided to trust him. 'Would this work with any horse?' she went on.

'What do you mean?' Sean was leading the mare

across the stable yard under the watchful eye of his father standing at the office window. The boy deliberately turned his back.

'Would you be able to "talk" to any horse like you just talked to this one? Does it always work?'

'I don't know for sure. All I can say is it's worked so far. I'd only been doing it for a few months before I went away to school. I'm still learning the signals. Like, I definitely know that if you look a horse in the eyes, he'll want to get as far away from you as he can.' Sean was about to launch into another explanation of his system as he opened a gate into a field behind the yard and led the mare in.

But Mandy's mind was working too fast to listen closely. They'd come to Lough Caher to find out more about Sean's special gift with horses. Their luck had been in and they'd actually seen him at work. He'd proved it without being asked. 'I expect you're wondering why we came,' she said now.

'To say sorry for yelling at me?' He'd forgotten his father's critical gaze as he turned the mare loose and watched her trot away with a half-grin on his face.

Mandy swallowed hard. 'Well, ye-es . . . partly!' She was ashamed that she and James had ever thought that Sean was the culprit who had put the headcollar on the foal.

Now he grinned properly. 'Me too. I'm sorry for being suspicious of you.'

'We're *all* sorry that Connie is still wearing that headcollar,' James pointed out. 'But being sorry doesn't get us very far. That's why we came to see you.'

'I don't know who did it,' Sean said quickly. 'I wish I did.'

'No, but we want to ask you to help,' Mandy said. 'James and I never really wanted to use the tranquilliser gun on the foal. We talked to my mum and dad about it, and they agreed that if there was another, gentler way to get near to Connie, it would be better.'

'Then we thought of you,' James told him.

'We heard you could talk to horses, and now we know you can!' Earnestly she persuaded Sean on to their side.

'That's why we want to know if you could do it with a wild pony,' James said. 'Could you?'

Sean closed the gate on the bay mare and gazed after her. For a while he wouldn't answer.

'Could you do it on Connie?' Mandy urged. 'Sean, would you at least try?'

'I hope he's not filling your head with his foolish ideas!' Before Sean could answer, Gerry Malone broke in with a scornful shout from across the yard. 'In any case, there's a whole list of chores for him to be getting on with.' He marched across to issue orders to his son.

'What's he got against Sean?' Mandy muttered to James.

James backed away from the towering figure of the horse-trainer as he stormed across. He'd already set his mind on the three-mile walk along the lakeside, across the flat, boggy stretch of land between Lough Caher and Drumcashel. 'I expect he thinks he knows best, that's all.'

And now Mandy had only seconds to prise an answer to her question out of the frowning boy. 'Will you come and work with Connie?' she whispered once more.

He muttered back as his father bore down on them. 'Tomorrow morning at eight o'clock, when the herd meets at the point to go down to drink. I'll be there,' he promised.

Six

'What's that strange yellow light in the sky?' Adam Hope joked, screwing up his face and shading his eyes as he opened the door to let in shafts of bright sunlight.

'See you later!' Mandy squeezed past him and set off for the cliff path. It was ten to eight on the following morning; almost time to meet Sean and go down to the beach.

'Where are you off to?' Her dad pretended to be dizzy and grasped the doorpost. 'What's the big rush?'

'Sean is going to talk to Connie!' James

exploded through the door after Mandy. 'We're going to try and get the headcollar off without using the gun!'

'Did he say "talk" to the foal?' Adam Hope asked his wife. Bemused, they stayed inside to finish breakfast.

But when Mandy and James reached the cliff point there was no sign of Sean Malone.

Eight o'clock came and went.

'Are we sure Sean hasn't already followed the ponies down?' James asked. It was quarter-past eight. He peered down the rocky path, across the empty white sands.

'He said he'd meet us here.' Mandy felt flat and empty. Sean had broken his word.

'We could try phoning him from the cottage,' James suggested. 'There's no point hanging round here if he's not going to come.'

They trudged back, unable to understand what had happened until they reached the cottage and saw a smart red Land-rover arrive. Out stepped a stern-looking Mr Malone.

'What does he want?' Mandy pulled back. Sean's father was the last person she would have expected to see.

They heard Emily Hope's surprised voice greet

the trainer, then heard Mr Malone introduce himself. Adam Hope invited him into the cottage. James and Mandy decided to hang around outside, listening without being seen.

'. . . I got it out of him in the end,' Gerry Malone told Emily and Adam Hope in his loud, firm voice. 'He told me about this injured Connemara foal; how your son and daughter had asked him to help . . .'

'James isn't our son,' Adam explained. 'He's our daughter's friend.'

Mr Malone ignored him. 'In any case, I soon put a stop to the idea. I grounded Sean for the day.'

Outside the door, James frowned. Mandy narrowed her eyes and stared angrily at the shiny red Land-rover.

'Wasn't that a bit harsh?' Emily Hope asked in a calm voice. 'After all, Sean was only responding to Mandy and James's request for help.'

The trainer tutted. 'I've told him before not to go spreading his foolish ideas. I've warned him that what he's doing is making a laughing-stock of me and the training yard.'

'I don't quite see how,' Adam Hope put in mildly.

'Good for you, Dad!' Mandy whispered.

'Don't you? Well, it flies in the face of all my methods of training horses, and I've no time for Sean's weird notions.'

'Maybe there's room for different ways of dealing with horses,' Mandy's mum suggested.

'I'm not denying it. But this talking to them business is what I can't stomach.' The trainer's voice grew even louder as he came back towards the door. His tone suggested that this was the end of the conversation.

'In any case, since I was driving over to see Tom O'Rourke at Kilmore Farm, I took it upon myself to call in and tell you why Sean wouldn't be here this morning.'

'Thank you,' Adam Hope said stiffly.

Malone appeared in the doorway. He spotted James and Mandy hovering outside. 'And to warn you that my son's a bit of a dreamer,' he went on, raising his voice another notch, casting a cold eye on Mandy. 'I'm afraid Sean will never make a horse trainer; not in a month of Sundays!'

'Well, *I* believe in Sean!' Mandy protested.

Gerry Malone had swept off towards the church in his Land-rover, leaving them at a loss. What should they do now? They went outside to talk it through.

'I'm not so sure.' James had been half-convinced by the trainer's views. 'Mr Malone must know an awful lot about horses,' he reminded her.

'But we saw Sean talk to the horse in the training ring at Lough Caher with our own eyes!'

They fell silent, each thinking their own thoughts.

'So, according to you, Mandy, Molloy wasn't exaggerating when he described what Sean can do?' Adam Hope wanted to be sure of the facts.

She shook her head. 'He can actually get a horse to do what he wants it to do without even touching it!' she insisted.

'How?' Emily Hope was interested to hear the details.

'By the way he stands and looks at it, by the way he uses his hands.' Mandy knew how it sounded; fanciful and unbelievable, but she'd seen Sean do it.

'We only saw it once,' James confessed. 'It could have been a one-off; pure luck.'

'Now you *do* sound like Sean's father!' Mandy said angrily, remembering the boy's earlier accusation.

'Let's not argue.' Mr Hope went inside for the car keys. 'I must say I'm intrigued. But I need to know a bit more about it before I'm convinced. Who fancies a drive over to Lough Caher with me?'

'What for?' Mandy felt drawn back to the cliff path, to see for herself how Rosie and Connie were getting on.

'I'd like to take a look around for myself,' her dad told her. 'Talk to a few of the people who work in the training yard while Gerry Malone isn't there.'

'I'll come,' James offered. 'I'll tell Sean we know why he couldn't make it.'

'I'll stay here,' Emily Hope decided. 'I fancy a sit in the sun with a good book.'

'Me too.' Privately, Mandy promised herself a trip down to the beach while James and her dad were gone.

But when she set off alone for the cliff path and read the signs of the hoofprints on the sand, she realised that the ponies had already come up off the beach. They'd followed their morning routine of drinking at Blackrock Pool and then they'd gone on their way.

'Too late!' she muttered to herself, studying the

direction of the prints. She lifted her gaze to the clifftops and scanned the breezy scene.

By now the sun was high in the clear sky. Banks of fuchsia hedges fringed the cliffs, fields rolled away inland like a giant patchwork quilt. On the next headland, the ruined stone church stood out almost white against the green and blue.

Mandy's gaze rested on the church and the broken crosses and unkempt mounds of the graves in the ancient churchyard. Movement there had attracted her attention. She saw without surprise that this was where the herd had made for when they came off the beach. They grazed quietly, heads down, moving gently between the tumbledown walls, through the old arched entrance.

Drawn towards them, Mandy set off to find Rosie and Connie. But she hadn't gone more than a hundred metres before she saw a figure running along the headland towards her. It was Sean Malone, a length of rope slung round his shoulder, leaping recklessly across a stream, stumbling over rocks in his effort to reach her.

'What are you doing here?' Mandy gasped, as soon as he was within earshot.

'Meeting you and James!' Sean scrambled

up the hill. 'What do you think?'

'Your father said he'd grounded you.'

He nodded. 'So?'

Mandy stared. Sean must have a strong nerve to defy Gerry Malone. 'How did you get here?'

'I walked. Sorry I'm late.' He caught his breath at last. 'Listen, I came by the church, and it's not good news!'

'What do you mean?' Mandy glanced back at the grazing herd of ponies.

'I looked for the lead mare and her foal . . .'

'Rosie and Connie.'

'. . . And I couldn't see them. They're not with the herd!'

'They must be!' Panic made Mandy set off at a run towards the church, but Sean cut her off.

'They're not, Mandy.' He made her stop and listen. 'That might mean they've been stolen. But to me it's more likely the foal got sick and the mare has stayed with her.'

'Too sick to move with the herd?' Slowly his words sank in. Mandy thought of zebra or deer in the wild. If a young one fell ill, the herd would move on to fresh pasture or to keep out of the way of predators, but the mother would stay to protect the sick youngster. Now Sean was saying that this was what Rosie might have done for Connie.

He nodded. 'Like you said; the wound on the foal's face could be infected and she's too weak to keep up. She could be in real trouble!'

'But where are they?' Mandy spun round to look, as if Rosie and Connie would suddenly appear.

'Did you see the ponies go down this morning?'

'No. Why?'

'This is just a guess,' Sean said, setting off again the way Mandy had come. 'But say the herd was still together overnight, with Rosie in charge as usual. Say she led them down to drink, but when it came to climbing back up the cliff path, the foal was too weak to make it . . . ?'

Mandy ran after him, realising that he was making for the path, which was the only way down to the long, curving stretch of sand below. 'So Rosie sent the herd on ahead, and they came up to graze in the churchyard, but she had to stay and wait for Connie?'

'Like I say, it's only a guess!' Grim-faced, Sean reached the path and began the dangerous descent. 'We've got to hurry. The tide's already coming in!'

Mandy glanced down at the surging waves as they smashed on to the beach. White spray foamed off the rocks on the headlands that stretched furthest out to sea. She felt her heart lurch as she realised that soon the water would swirl up the sands and into the narrow inlets of the bay.

'How long have we got?' she asked, as finally they jumped the last couple of metres on to the beach.

'An hour, maybe a bit longer.' Sean crouched to study the hoofprints. 'These must be fresh because the waves haven't washed them away yet!'

The prints curved across the sand and converged at the point below the path; evidence that the herd had followed the normal pattern.

Still there was no proof that Sean's theory was right, until Mandy spotted two sets of prints separate from the rest. One set was smaller than the other; those of a foal following in the steps of its mother. And these prints wandered here and there across the beach. They were scuffed and uneven, as if the young pony was dragging her feet.

'Let's follow them!' Mandy went ahead, noticing where the tracks churned up the sand and seemed

to follow tight circles before setting off again towards Kilmore Cove. Behind her, she heard the sea's constant roar as the giant waves flung themselves against the shore.

'Over here!' Sean took a short cut towards the narrow inlet. He'd picked up the trail again.

Mandy began to run. 'What happens when the tide comes in?' she gasped. Glancing over her shoulder, she saw that it was happening faster than she'd imagined. 'It comes all the way up the beach, doesn't it?'

Yesterday, in the cave, her dad had pointed out

the stranded seaweed and debris that the sea had left behind.

Sean nodded. 'And there's no other way out, if that's what you're thinking. Once the tide comes past the point, we're trapped!'

'And so are Rosie and Connie!' Mandy picked up speed, convinced now that this was where the mare had taken refuge with the sick foal. The cliffs of Kilmore Cove rose sheer to either side, and narrowed to the cave at the far end. Still she searched desperately for the two ponies.

'There they are!' She spotted them at last.

Rosie stood guard over Connie, and it was just as they'd feared; a fever had set in. The foal lay against a boulder by Blackrock Pool. She was on her side, her thin legs folded under her, hardly able to lift her head. The strawberry roan mare nuzzled and pushed with her nose, urging her to get up. When she heard Mandy and Sean and saw them round the corner, she stamped her feet and gave a shrill cry.

'What do we do?' Mandy stopped dead. To go on now would mean frightening Connie and angering the mare. Her heart went out to the weak foal. The wounds on her face were covered in sand. She struggled to her knees, then collapsed on to her side once more.

Sean looked up at the natural barriers of the rocks to either side, fingering the rope he wore across his shoulder. He and Mandy stood at a spot in the inlet where the walls of rock formed a bottleneck only twenty metres or so wide. 'See how this is a kind of corral?' he said quickly.

She nodded. 'We've got them trapped.'

'So, you stand here. You're a sentry, right? If the mare tries to escape, you don't let her.'

Mandy stared at him. 'You want me to keep her in here?'

'Yes. Don't let her out. I don't think she'll leave the foal in any case. But if she does, you have to stop her!'

Taking a deep breath, she agreed. 'Be quick!' she whispered, standing with her back to the sea, trying to block the roar of the waves as the tide rushed in.

So Sean went into the natural arena of rock and sand, arms stretched wide, fingers spread. He challenged Rosie, sending her fleeing around the edge of the sandy ring, keeping one eye on him, one on her sick foal.

Mandy watched impatiently. When Rosie came round her section of the arena, she stood her ground. She felt the sand shake under the wild pony's drumming hooves. 'Why don't you try to get near to Connie?' she yelled to Sean. While the mare thundered round the ring, she left the foal apparently unprotected.

'If I do, she'll knock me flat,' Sean replied, never for a second taking his eyes off the mare. 'She'd kill me to save the foal!'

Still Rosie careered on. Her wet mane flapped against her hot neck, her feet sank deep into the sand. Mandy could see the flecks of sweat on her neck and withers as she came round one more time.

Four, five, six times, she made a circle round the foot of the cliffs. By now she had her inside ear locked on to Sean, who stood in the centre of the space, about ten paces from Connie. Then the mare's head went down as she ran, she began to move her bottom jaw in a chewing motion.

'See that!' Sean followed her with his body, turning on the spot. 'She's ready to talk!'

'Let it not be a fluke,' Mandy prayed. 'Please let him be right!' All the doubts that Gerry Malone had voiced flew to the surface as Sean went on working intently with the mare.

He let his gaze slide from Rosie's face, down

her neck to her shoulder. The mare slowed to a walk. With a wary eye on her foal, she stepped in towards the boy.

'Good girl!' he said quietly, eyes averted, letting the wild creature come right in.

Mandy held her breath. She saw Sean turn away from Rosie, saw the mare hesitate, then decide to follow. He made an arc with her to the left, then to the right. Then he stopped, and still without looking her in the face, he reached up to rub Rosie between the eyes.

'Watch her now. She's going to let me run my hands over her neck,' he predicted. 'She trusts me a little bit. She knows I'm not going to harm her.'

'Quickly!' Mandy breathed. Minutes were ticking by. The roar of the tide grew louder.

Sean ran his hands over the mare's neck and shoulders. Then he eased them over her back with a light, rubbing motion. Mandy saw him crook one hand towards the rope and lift it over his head, ready for use. The mare's ear flicked towards the moving hand. She quivered . . .

And then she shied and was away; back at the rim of the arena. And Sean had to begin again, challenging her, driving her round the ring, making her want to come back in and talk.

Mandy almost cried. So near, yet so far. She glanced at Connie collapsed in the sand, heard the waves threaten, closer and closer.

But Sean didn't panic. He knew what would happen; that this time the mare would read his signals more quickly and want to come in and talk sooner than before. She cantered round the circle two . . . three times, then her head went down and she was in talking mood.

The boy let her in. He rewarded her with a rub between the eyes. And before she had time to object, he gently slipped the halter round her neck.

Seven

'She knows we're her friends,' Sean said quietly.

Rosie didn't strain at the halter. She stood placidly, waiting for Sean and Mandy to take the lead.

Mandy realised the tide was rising fast. The first waves had reached the outcrops of rock that bordered the cove. Already they would have to wade the ponies to freedom.

She went and kneeled beside Connie. 'She's too weak to stand. We'll have to carry her,' she suggested.

'Let Rosie do it.' Sean led the mare across. She

came anxiously, nosing at her foal, urging her to get up once more. 'The mare can take the foal's weight across her back,' he decided.

Connie lifted her head, and Mandy could see that the wounds were red and raw where the ropes cut into her nose and chin. Sand had worked its way in, and the deep, savage cuts had begun to weep infected pus. Mandy winced. 'Shall we lift her together?'

Sean nodded. He let go of Rosie's halter while he and Mandy stooped to lift Connie. The mare stood quite still, as if she understood the plan. Then they laid the unprotesting foal across the mother's broad shoulders. She took the weight.

'Good girl,' Mandy breathed. She rubbed Rosie's nose. Keeping a steadying hand on Connie, she felt Sean take up the halter rope and begin to lead them out of the cove.

The pony stepped slowly towards the crashing waves, careful of her burden. As she swayed from side to side, Connie would shift slightly, so Mandy kept her hand in place, steadying the foal as the mare walked forward.

'We should just make it!' Sean muttered. An advance wave smashed against a nearby rock, showering them with spray.

Rosie shook her head as the water splashed all around them. Her dappled coat grew dark. But she trod steadily on, following Sean's lead. Together they waded into the swirling, foaming shallows of the mighty ocean.

'Not long now!' Mandy promised Connie. The foal struggled feebly to raise her head, but then she sank back against her mother's shoulders. Her eyes were half-closed, her strength almost spent.

Then they rounded the spit of land and turned their backs on the greedy waves, to head up the beach as fast as they could towards the cliff path.

'Mandy, Sean!' A voice called them from the clifftop. It was Emily Hope, waving and yelling at the top of her voice. She could see the waves gaining on them as they toiled up the beach with Connie.

'It's OK, Mum. We're fine!' Mandy yelled back. 'We'll make it, don't worry!'

Sean led Rosie over the soft sand. When they reached the path, he turned, gritted his teeth and gently slid the foal from her mother's back. 'This is too steep to manage. I'll have to lead the mare to the top,' he told Mandy. 'You wait here with the foal and I'll come back to help you carry her up.'

Fear grabbed at her, but Mandy nodded. What if the waves caught up with her and Connie as they waited? The force of one giant breaker could sweep them off their feet and drag them out of their depth.

From above, Emily Hope saw Sean and Rosie begin to toil up the path alone. 'I'm coming down!' she yelled.

'OK!' Mandy was relieved. Her mum could help her with Connie. She watched the red-haired figure begin to scramble towards them, as Sean and Rosie climbed the steep slope. As their paths crossed, the mare skittered sideways and pulled at the halter. Sean held tight and the danger passed. Then Emily Hope's way down was clear. She came quickly, half-sliding and grabbing at the roots of bushes to steady herself.

'Right, Mandy, let's try and stretcher the foal up out of here!' she said as she arrived at the foot of the cliff. Rapidly she took off her jacket. 'We can improvise with this . . . make a kind of sling to take her weight.'

She worked as she talked, sliding the jacket under Connie and handing Mandy one sleeve and a corner to hold, while she took the other end.

Just in time. The waves foamed at their feet,

white spray showered them. There was the suck and pull of a mighty natural force as each wave ebbed and the next one surged over it.

But they were moving, leaving the sea behind, climbing the path and gaining height.

Mandy edged backwards up the slope, hanging on to her two corners of the sling. They crept to safety. Before they reached the top, she saw that Drumcashel beach had disappeared under the waves. They'd made it with only minutes to spare.

Word had got round; there were people and ponies stranded on the beach. Locals from the villages and farms came to see if help was needed. Molloy left his shop and ran the length of the main street, gathering more assistance. He arrived at the clifftop with a dozen men, women and children.

'Is there anyone else down there?' he asked anxiously as he headed towards the crowd gathered round Sean and the strawberry roan mare.

'Mandy and her mother are on their way up with the foal,' he told them. He waited until he saw they were safe, then he moved Rosie away from the crowd, towards the rest of the herd who stood uneasily at a distance, in the grounds of the old church.

'Stand back!' Molloy took charge. 'Give the vet room! Go on, there; move away!'

He spoke harshly to the driver of the Land-rover that had pulled up at the scene. The vehicle crowded in much too close to the onlookers before two men jumped out. It was Gerry Malone and Tom O'Rourke, the farmer from Kilmore Farm. They ignored the shopkeeper and pushed through to the front, just as Mandy and Emily Hope finally reached the top of the path with their sick foal.

'Now, don't panic!' Molloy insisted. 'The crisis is over and no one has been hurt, thank goodness. Your boy, Sean, has brought the mare to safety.'

'What's Sean doing here?' Gerry Malone looked round in irritation. But he was too caught up in Mandy and Mrs Hope's rescue of the foal to follow up his query. 'What's wrong with her anyway?' Again he muscled his way forward, followed by the burly figure of O'Rourke.

'See where this headcollar has cut into her face?' Emily Hope showed them the damage as she and Mandy gently laid the foal on the grass.

At last Molloy managed to push people back

into a circle and bring order. 'Is there anything we can do?'

'We need scissors or a knife to cut the rope . . .' Mrs Hope inspected the discharge from the wounds with a frown. 'Try the cottage.'

'No need.' Mandy slipped her hand into her pocket and drew out the penknife she'd put there the day before.

'OK, Mandy, you work on that while I run for my bag,' Emily decided. 'We'll need antibiotics, swabs to clean the wounds . . .' She was already on her feet, pushing through the crowd and running for the cottage.

Mandy opened up the knife. She tried to slip her fingertips between the headcollar and Connie's cheek, but the rope was much too tight. So gently and carefully she began to saw away at the rope that went behind the foal's ears, across the bony poll that was cushioned by the thick black mane.

'Easy does it!' Molloy breathed. He held off Gerry Malone to give Mandy breathing space.

'Who put the collar on in the first place?' the trainer asked. 'Isn't this one of the park ponies?'

People in the crowd grunted and nodded. They asked Tom O'Rourke if he'd spotted anything from his clifftop farm, but he said he was too busy working to be keeping an eye on the wild ponies all the time. It was a mystery; no one knew anything about the headcollar.

'It's against the law to catch a wild pony,' a woman said. 'They belong to the national park. Which means, in a way, they belong to all of us!'

'Maybe this was done by outsiders,' someone else murmured. 'We know there are illegal traders in the area.'

'I don't know about that. But I do know it's cruel,' Molloy pointed out.

Meanwhile, Mrs Hope came running back with her bag of instruments. She crouched beside Mandy and the foal.

'It's nearly through.' Mandy concentrated on the frayed rope. Now only a few threads held the cruel headcollar in place. Gently she sawed with the blade until these too frayed and snapped.

'Lovely!' Emily Hope nodded and slipped the headcollar over Connie's ears. The filthy rope came away at last. 'There, that must feel better!' She soothed the patient, who lay on the grass and tried to raise her head.

Mandy took a deep breath. Now her mum got

to work to give Connie injections that would cure the infection.

Emily Hope took her patient's temperature and checked her all over for signs of other problems. Then she cleaned the wounds on the foal's face with swabs of cotton wool. 'Pass me the antibiotic spray, please,' she told Mandy. 'This will help dry up the wounds and give extra protection against infection,' she explained.

'That's great.' Molloy bent over, hands on his knees, studying the vet's work. When the spray came out bright blue and dyed the bridge of the foal's nose the colour of the sky, he grinned. 'We can see her coming now, and no mistake!'

'Well, we will need to keep an eye on her for a few days, won't we, Mum?' Mandy knew that Connie's injuries wouldn't heal overnight. And the foal would still be weak from the infection.

'Hmm.' Satisfied that they'd done all they could, Emily Hope packed her bag. 'I suppose the best thing would be to keep both the mare and the foal in a nearby field until we're satisfied that she's strong enough to go back to the herd.'

There was a murmur of agreement among the crowd.

'Will they stay put?' Mandy wondered. 'Won't they try to escape?' She glanced across the grassy bank towards the church, where Sean stood with Rosie. Behind them, the herd had gathered in a restless, uneasy knot. Somehow it felt wrong to be thinking of shutting the lead mare in a field.

'It won't be for long,' her mum reassured her. 'And I can't see the mare being happy to leave the foal by herself, can you?'

'No.' After what had happened on the beach, Mandy had to agree. Rosie would risk anything to stay with Connie.

'You need a nice, quiet field with a good fence,' Molloy warned.

'Or a big hedge,' Gerry Malone cut in. 'Tom

here has just the field, don't you, Tom?'

The farmer was slow to answer. 'I've no time to waste . . .' he began. But a sharp look from the trainer made him change his mind. 'I suppose you mean the field overlooking the beach?' he grumbled.

'By the point,' Gerry confirmed. 'Isn't that surrounded on three sides by fuchsia hedges?'

Tom O'Rourke nodded. 'And the fourth side drops clean away to the beach.'

'What do you think?' Mandy asked her mum. For some reason, the offer from the farmer didn't come across as sincere. 'Would it be a good place?'

Emily Hope stood up straight and surveyed the church headland. 'It sounds secure enough.' She too seemed doubtful. 'And it does have the advantage of overlooking Kilmore Cove, doesn't it? I suppose the ponies will be reasonably happy if they can see their own beach.'

'Will you mind us coming to visit them?' Mandy asked the farmer. She would worry if Rosie and Connie couldn't be checked.

'How often?' Mr O'Rourke asked grudgingly.

'A couple of times a day.' Mrs Hope watched Mandy stroke the foal's neck. 'To take her temperature and so on.'

'That'll be no problem, will it, Tom?' Gerry Malone seemed keen to get the decision made.

He probably wants to get his hands on Sean, Mandy thought. She didn't envy her new friend when his father got him home.

'It had better not put me to extra trouble.' Still the tall, surly farmer hesitated.

'Shame!' someone in the crowd muttered.

'Show a drop of generosity for once, Tom!' Molloy said.

So at last the farmer's field by the cliff was settled on as the place where Connie would convalesce. Tom O'Rourke was persuaded to bring his trailer to carry the invalid to his farm, while Mandy left her mum with Connie and went across the fields to explain the latest events to Sean.

'Sean!' She had to call across the ruined churchyard, into the shell of the old stone building and through the other side. To her surprise, the boy had vanished with Rosie.

'Where are you?' Her voice echoed up through the roofless church. She was surrounded by overgrown graves, crooked stone crosses . . . and watching eyes.

The wild ponies stood waiting and looking on.

The sun beat down on their broad backs, their tails whisked and their ears twitched to drive off the flies. Through a narrow arched window at the far end of the church, she glimpsed the strawberry roan.

Mandy ran to the window. She found Sean standing with Rosie by the large cross that overlooked the sea.

'Why didn't you answer?' she asked.

'You found us anyway.' He didn't turn to look at her. Something on the horizon seemed to draw his attention.

The mare stamped her foot and shook her head. Her hoof caught on a stone slab. The noise grated in the peaceful silence.

'Mum says Connie will need more treatment.'

'I know.'

'How?'

'I suppose I just guessed. Rosie will have to stay with her.' Sean's voice sounded flat and strangely defeated.

'Just for a few days.' Now she sounded like her mum, she realised. 'I don't like it either,' she confessed. 'If we put Rosie and Connie into Mr O'Rourke's field, it might feel like we're betraying them somehow.' These ponies were wild; they'd never been penned in a field before.

'Tom O'Rourke?' Sean wheeled round to stare at her. His sudden action made Rosie start and quiver.

Mandy stepped back. 'Yes. Why not?'

When Sean wouldn't answer, she went on. 'As a matter of fact, it was your father's idea.'

Instinctively the boy's hand went to the pony's neck. He turned away with Rosie, across the churchyard.

'Where are you going? Stop, Sean! You can't take Rosie with you!' Mandy ran to catch him up. She stumbled on a fallen stone, picked herself up and followed again. Behind her, the herd of wild ponies began to move off along the cliff.

'Mr O'Rourke's gone for a trailer to take Connie back with him!' she pleaded. 'We want Rosie to go into the field with her. Sean, come back. Connie will need her mother to help her get better!'

'Just remember, whatever you may think of Tom O'Rourke, he's still a great man for the horses!' Molloy stood in the churchyard, helping Sean to see reason.

The shopkeeper had seen Mandy struggling to

persuade the boy to bring the mare to the farmer's field. He'd left the knot of curious onlookers and come to lend a hand.

Sean held fast to Rosie's halter, scowling across at the trailer as O'Rourke towed it to where Emily Hope waited with the foal.

'Admit it, now; you can't fault Tom's knowledge of the horses.' Molloy waited for the trainer's son to calm down. The mare was as edgy as he was, and the whole herd stamped and snorted impatiently by the tumbledown churchyard wall.

'I don't like this either,' Mandy admitted. 'I hate to see Rosie and Connie cooped up in a field when they should be running free. But Rosie trusts us now, and I reckon she's clever enough to see we're doing it for Connie.'

'They'll be in good hands,' Molloy promised. 'That's a fine vet we have over there.' He gestured towards Emily Hope, who was supervising the lifting of Connie into the trailer. The foal was still weak, so Mrs Hope was insisting on a thick bed of straw for her to lie on. 'I've seen plenty of vets in my time, and believe me, she knows what she's doing.'

Mandy gave him a grateful smile. Then she turned to plead with a silent, sullen Sean once more. 'Mum says Connie will need treatment for a few days. But after that, she should be completely better; strong enough to go back with the herd, as if none of this had ever happened.'

By now the trailer ramp was up, with Connie and Emily Hope inside. Rosie was beginning to strain at the halter, afraid of what was happening to her foal.

'Let's walk her across to Church Farm,' Mandy suggested. Beyond the church headland, the cliffs dropped back into another sheltered bay. There was a low stone farm building in a tree-lined hollow, a few hundred metres from where they stood. They would be able to keep the trailer in sight as Mr O'Rourke drove it back home.

'Why is he doing this?' Sean spoke through gritted teeth. He steadied Rosie with one hand as they turned to watch the trailer's progress. 'When did Mr O'Rourke ever do anyone round here a favour?'

Surprised by the fierceness of his voice, Mandy grimaced.

But Molloy grinned. 'We all put the pressure on him to do the decent thing for once. Yes, I know it's not easy to believe, but he did actually agree to give up his field for a few days. So come on, what do you say? Shall we put this mare out of her misery and take her to see her foal?'

Sean gave the tiniest nod imaginable. Slowly, reluctantly, he gave in. He stroked Rosie between the eyes, then flicked his hand over her neck.

He led her on, picking his way through the grassy mounds and gravestones, down the hill towards Church Farm.

Eight

For two days, through Tuesday and Wednesday, the herd of wild ponies grazed on the open hillsides without Rosie to lead them.

Mandy and James would seek them out on the peatland behind Drumcashel village, or down on the windy beach. They came across them again in the mist on a warm morning, as they rode on hired bikes towards the Benmore mountains.

'There's the rebel grey pony!' Mandy pointed out the troublesome youngster wandering away from the herd and getting himself bogged down in soft ground near a stream at the foot of the deep purple hills. He pulled himself clear, but his sturdy legs were clogged with mud.

'That would never have happened if Rosie had been here to boss him around!' James grinned.

Standing astride her mountain bike, Mandy picked out the piebald pony, the dun mare and her tiny foal. 'Not long now!' She promised them that Rosie and Connie would soon be back with them, before she and James set off for Lough Caher to see Sean.

'He's not here.' Gerry Malone intercepted them at the gate. He leaned out of his smart red Land-rover to stop them cycling up the drive. 'So no point wasting your time.'

James braked hard to avoid Mr Malone. They hadn't seen Sean since he'd slipped the halter from Rosie's neck and left her in Tom O'Rourke's field. He'd gone off then without a word.

'Could you tell him that Connie's a lot better, please?' Mandy asked. 'Mum says the antibiotics have cleared up the infection. She's getting her strength back, and she'll soon be ready to leave the farm.'

The trainer nodded. He hadn't even bothered to stop the car, but swept on up the road before she'd finished.

'And Rosie's fine too!' Mandy shouted after him, annoyed. 'If anybody round here cares about the wild ponies, say there's no need to worry. Everything's fine!'

'. . . We hope!' James added.

Mandy and James went with Emily Hope to Church Farm to visit the patient that Wednesday evening.

Mrs Hope had finished off the course of antibiotic injections and pronounced the foal free of infection. 'Temperature's normal,' she told them. 'The wounds have healed over nicely. Connie is well on the road to a complete recovery!'

Mandy and James stayed on in Mr O'Rourke's field to chat with the ponies. They promised to follow Mandy's mum down to Molloys.

'There's going to be live music in the pub tonight,' Emily Hope told them. 'I hear Molloy himself plays a mean fiddle!'

'We'll be there in half an hour,' James promised.

But the light, warm summer evening tempted them to stay longer. The field, surrounded on three sides by high, flowering hedges, overlooked the bay, and this far edge of the enclosure was

Rosie and Connie's favourite spot. From there they could look down on their beach, watch the herd come and go to Kilmore Cove, and let their heads be filled with the sound of the sea.

'Not long now!' Mandy delivered the same promise that she'd given the herd by the Benmore mountains. Connie let her come close and put an arm around her neck. Rosie stood nearby. The wind blew her dark brown mane against her strong neck as she turned her face from the shore and kept a watchful eye on Mandy and Connie.

'Wouldn't it be wonderful?' Mandy whispered. She felt proud that the two wild ponies had learned to trust them.

'Wouldn't what be wonderful?' James sat on the grass with his back to her, looking out at the sunset.

'If we could learn to do what Sean does with them.' At night, when she lay in bed, Mandy went over what it was that the boy did when he spoke to these beautiful creatures. 'I mean, there's nothing mysterious when you think about it. It's practical; based on knowing a lot about horses. A kind of body language.'

'Yeah.' From the start, James had been doubtful. True, he'd seen the demonstration in the training arena, but that could have been a one-off, he still insisted. But he hadn't been there to see Sean save Rosie and Connie from the cove, even though Mandy had talked non-stop about it ever since. 'Are you ready? Shall we go to Molloys?'

She ignored him. 'I'd love to do it.' She gazed at Rosie's perfect face; small and neat, with the dark mane blowing across her forehead.

'Pity Sean isn't around to teach you, then.' James stood up suddenly and brushed loose grass from his jeans. He startled Connie, who pulled away from Mandy and ran to her mother's side.

'James?' Mandy frowned. 'What's wrong?'

'I said, it's a pity you can't ask Sean Malone more about this magic system of his.'

'It's not magic. It's common sense.' She ran after James as he strode across the field towards the gate.

'Whatever. But if he's so mad keen on these ponies, like they say, why hasn't he been to visit Connie and Rosie these last two days?'

'I don't know!' Mandy ran ahead of him, then turned and ran backwards as she spoke. 'I suppose it's because he hates Mr O'Rourke!'

'That wouldn't stop him if he really cared about the ponies, would it?' James was scornful. There was a deep frown line between his eyes.

Mandy came to a halt against the gate. She stopped James from opening it. 'Maybe his dad's grounded him again!'

'It didn't stop him last time!' Seeing that Mandy barred his way, James sidestepped her and climbed over the gate. 'I'm going back to the cottages,' he muttered from the far side. 'I don't feel like sitting round in Molloys all night listening to more stuff about brilliant Sean Malone!'

'Isn't James feeling well?' Adam Hope asked, above the noise of a violin, two flutes, a tambourine and a clarinet.

Mandy ducked her head and blushed. 'That's not exactly the problem.'

'Ah!' Her father thought he'd guessed what it was. 'He doesn't fancy traditional Irish music, eh?'

She shrugged and sighed, gazing round at the happy faces. Molloys was crowded and warm. Molloy himself had left his usual station behind the bar, had taken up his fiddle and was standing alongside the other foot-tapping musicians.

'Maybe James was embarrassed by the idea of you getting up to sing!' Emily Hope said with a grin. 'That's what your father's been threatening to do,' she whispered to Mandy in mock horror.

Mandy's dad cleared his throat and practised a few notes of the song that the band was playing. ' "When Irish eyes are smiling . . . all the world seems bright and gay . . ." '

'Oh no!' Mandy groaned. Her dad had a nice voice; he sang in the Welford church choir. But that was different from making a show of himself here. Trust him to get everyone in the room staring at them.

'Later, perhaps!' Emily Hope put a restraining hand on his arm.

But Molloy had heard the short rehearsal. He stepped out of the knot of musicians and hauled Adam Hope to his feet. 'That's a grand voice you have there!' he announced.

All heads turned. Mandy felt her face go beetroot red.

'Come on, now. Stand up with us and sing!' The barkeeper wouldn't take no for an answer.

As he dragged Adam Hope across the room, to the applause of other customers, Mandy made a quick getaway.

'I'm just going outside for a breath of fresh air,' she said to her mum.

She was through the crowd and out of the pub

before her dad could sing a note. 'Phew!' She leaned against the cool stone wall and gazed down the empty street. It seemed that everyone in Drumcashel was in Molloys listening to the band. Strains of the next song drifted through the door.

Not quite everyone . . . Mandy noticed Gerry Malone's recognisable red Land-rover; smarter and newer than most of the battered farm vehicles round here. The trainer sat inside with the thickset figure of Tom O'Rourke. The two men were in deep conversation.

'. . . This makes no difference,' Mr Malone was saying.

Mandy strained to hear through the open window. But she stayed well-hidden behind a muddy, battered old tractor parked outside the pub doorway.

'Listen, the money I lost at the races last month has left me short of cash for the business. So the plan to take six ponies and sell them goes ahead anyway. Why shouldn't it?' Malone sounded impatient and abrupt as ever.

'Because I've got two of them on my land, that's why not!' O'Rourke's deeper voice was slow and stubborn. 'If they vanish into thin air, people are bound to suspect me!'

Mandy frowned. What did Sean's father mean: 'take six ponies'?

'It wasn't a good idea of yours to push the injured foal and the mare on to me,' O'Rourke complained. 'I noticed how keen you were to put them in my field. But I thought at the time it was a wrong move.'

'Rubbish. We'd earmarked the strawberry roan as one of the six, hadn't we? She's a nice mare. We'll get a good price from a stables for her.'

Again Mandy strained to hear and understand. Hard as it was to believe, it sounded as if Gerry Malone was talking about Rosie.

He went on. 'Listen, Tom, we've been careful to cover our tracks by putting around that story about foreign horse thieves. And by taking in the sick foal and the mare, people are bound to think that you have the animals' welfare at heart.'

O'Rourke grunted. 'Maybe. But I'm telling you one thing; if we do go ahead and steal them, we're not offering these ponies to a stables anywhere in Connemara. It's too close to home. Word is bound to get around that a bunch of wild ponies has been stolen, and no one in the west of Ireland will want anything to do with them.'

There was a silence. Mandy pressed against the

side of the tractor, stunned by what she'd heard.

'You're not getting cold feet, are you?' Malone sneered.

'Quiet. I'm thinking,' O'Rourke barked back. 'It's one thing taking an odd foal or two out of a herd every now and then. No one notices that, except your son, maybe.'

'Hmm.' It was Malone's turn to stay quiet.

'He's got eyes in the back of his head,' the farmer complained. 'It's a good job he was away at school when I put that headcollar on the chestnut foal in the first place. Then the slippery little thing goes and escapes, doesn't she? Well, it was the mare who came for me as soon as I'd got the collar fastened, as you know. You saw how she reared up. I'd no choice but to let the foal go.'

'You'll have to be more careful this time,' the trainer agreed. 'But in any case, no one suspected you on that occasion, did they? So what makes you think they'll suspect this time; especially if I keep my son out of the way, as I plan to do?'

'Because we're not talking just one or two foals this time, are we? We're talking about six full-grown ponies!'

Mandy gasped and held on to the tractor wheel.

Now she understood the full extent of Malone and O'Rourke's betrayal. Neither of them cared one little bit about the wild ponies. Quite the opposite; they would capture them and sell them without a second thought.

'Six juicy profits from the sale of the ponies to a stables a long way from here,' Sean's father insisted. 'Money to help me out of a desperate financial difficulty; otherwise the yard might have to close. Money to help set you up with a new tractor . . . !'

As the trainer turned to the old tractor she was hiding behind, Mandy bobbed out of sight.

'Hmm. Maybe you're right.' The temptation was proving too strong for the farmer to resist. 'But let's get it over and done with as quick as we can.'

'Good man. How about first thing tomorrow for the strawberry roan?' Malone's voice was triumphant.

'Then the piebald and the young grey when the herd goes down to the beach,' O'Rourke agreed. He spoke rapidly, opening the door to the Land-rover, and stepping out on to the pavement. 'You're sure your lad isn't going to try and interfere?'

Mandy crept away from the shelter of

O'Rourke's old tractor as he headed towards it. She didn't want them to spot her now.

'I packed him off to Galway on Monday. He's staying in town with his aunt until I send for him.'

'Then there's the busybody kids staying at Cashel Cottages,' the farmer reminded Malone.

'You'd better load the roan out of the field into the trailer at the crack of dawn, before they're awake,' the trainer decided.

'Huh! I notice you say "you",' O'Rourke grumbled. 'There's no chance of getting you to dirty your own hands, is there?'

'It would attract attention to have me over at your place at that time in the morning,' the trainer argued. 'I'll be ready and waiting at Lough Caher, don't you worry. After you've got the mare, try for the two colts on their way down to drink.'

He started up his engine and backed the Land-rover on to the road. 'I'll get a stable ready for them at my place. That's my part of the bargain. I'll hide them there for a day or two, while you catch three more.'

'And you'll look for a buyer?'

Mandy squeezed into the pub doorway as O'Rourke climbed into the cab of his tractor.

'I already have one or two in mind. Some stables

just outside Dublin. They're always on the lookout for good quality hacking ponies, no questions asked.'

As the two horse thieves made their final plans, Mandy sank back inside the bar. The music had stopped, people were on their feet applauding. Her dad was looking flushed and happy as he took his bow. But she saw it all in a daze.

She thought of Rosie snatched from the field overlooking the beach, bundled into a dark trailer and driven over to Lough Caher. She pictured the long drive to Dublin; the herd left behind without its leader.

'And Connie!' she gasped out loud. Malone and O'Rourke hadn't mentioned the foal. 'What's going to happen to her if they get away with this?'

Nine

'We have to stop them!' James said quietly.

Although they'd argued, Mandy had decided to share with James what she'd overheard outside Molloys. She'd hardly been able to wait for the musical evening to end before she and her mum and dad came back to Cashel Cottages. James had been reading at the kitchen table. He looked up with a shrug, as if to say sorry about the stupid row.

'How?' Mandy's head was spinning. Her mum and dad were in the lounge, sitting with their feet up in front of the television.

'We could go to the police.' This was the logical thing to do to stop the horse thieves.

'But, as Mum and Dad would tell us, they haven't actually done anything wrong yet!' Mandy could hear their very words; 'How can you report a crime *before* it's been committed?'

'We could get Sean to help us.' For James, this was a hard suggestion to make. 'I'm sorry I was rotten about him earlier,' he added.

Mandy nodded quickly. 'That's OK. I know Sean would be able to think of something, but his father's sent him away to Galway.' She paused to think. 'Really, Sean is in a terrible position.'

'Do you think he knows about his father and O'Rourke?' James asked.

'I don't know if he realises that his dad's involved,' Mandy answered. 'Or if he knows about O'Rourke either. He was away when all this first started, remember. But he definitely doesn't trust him.'

'No. He didn't want us to leave Rosie and Connie in O'Rourke's field!'

'Yes. And since he didn't tell anyone about it, that makes me pretty sure that he might suspect that his dad's involved in all this!' Mandy stopped to think again. 'He wouldn't have been able to turn his own father in to the police, would he?'

'Yet he cares so much about the ponies.' James realised how Sean must have been pulled in two.

'In any case, will you get up with me at dawn tomorrow?' Mandy pleaded. 'Whatever else happens, we've got to keep Rosie out of O'Rourke's hands!'

'We'll wait until the last minute!' James whispered, next morning. 'And then, when we can actually see O'Rourke trying to get Rosie into a trailer, we'll have the proof we need.'

A low, white mist clung to the hillside. It was damp and dense, rolling in from the sea.

'You can attract his attention and distract him from Rosie while I run for my mum and dad.' Mandy went over the plan they'd made.

When she'd told him the full story of what she'd heard outside the pub, James had cast away all his doubts about Sean. Now he was well and truly on her side. But Mandy shivered as they crouched behind the tall hedge, waiting for the rumble of a Land-rover engine; the tell-tale sign that the farmer was on his way.

'Can you see Rosie and Connie in the field?' James asked. Mist swirled over the rough, tussocky grass and drenched hundreds of cobwebs woven from branch to branch of the fuchsia bushes. They glistened and dripped in the first rays of morning sun.

'Over by the cliff.' Mandy peered through a gap in the hedge. She could make out two grey shapes in the distance. The ponies stood without moving a muscle, heads up, ears pricked.

'Can you hear that?' James picked up the sound of the dreaded approach of O'Rourke's Land-rover from the direction of the farmhouse. Behind it, an empty trailer bumped and rattled over the rough ground.

Mandy felt her heart thump. She ducked behind the hedge, praying that between them, she and James would be able to stop O'Rourke and let the whole village know about him and the crooked trainer.

'Look!' Through a gap low down in the hedge, James pointed to the Land-rover and trailer as O'Rourke backed it into the gateway.

Across the field, Rosie shepherded her foal into the furthest corner. She evidently didn't like the look of the farmer's vehicle, and stood guard between it and Connie, ready to attack if need be. Connie peered out from behind her mother, front legs splayed, head down and stretched forward.

They saw O'Rourke step down from the Land-rover, rope in hand. He entered the field and strode purposefully towards the mare and foal. He clutched a whip in the other hand, resting half out of sight of Rosie, but ready for use if she resisted.

'Oh!' Mandy almost sprang up and shouted when she saw the whip. This was too cruel for words.

They saw Rosie try to edge her foal away from the cliff as the farmer came at the two ponies. She tossed her head and half reared up, warning him to keep his distance.

O'Rourke wielded the whip. It snaked towards the mare and sent her reeling back. Connie retreated, getting closer to the sheer drop over the cliff.

'Get back!' The farmer cracked the whip and forced the mare and foal apart.

'What's he trying to do?' James muttered, hanging on to Mandy to stop her from jumping up out of hiding.

'It looks like he's trying to drive her over the cliff!' Mandy could hardly bear to look. 'She's in the way, so he's going to get rid of her!' Even in her worst nightmare, she could never have pictured this.

O'Rourke moved in on the defenceless young pony, towering over her, holding the whip above her head.

Connie backed off. The cliff face was only metres away. Rosie opened her mouth and squealed a warning.

'Quiet!' O'Rourke wheeled round clumsily. He slashed the whip towards the mare.

In the distance, answering squeals came from the direction of the churchyard; the shrill, sharp cries of ponies who sense danger.

Rosie was up again on her hind legs, her front hooves beating the air. She wanted to draw the attacker's attention away from Connie, and she was succeeding. O'Rourke had to leave the foal and try to silence the mare.

He lunged at her, flicking the long whip, turning her aside as the tip bit into her face.

Now Mandy couldn't contain herself. She stood up from behind the hedge.

Rosie reared and whinnied in pain. She felt the lash of the whip a second time, must have seen the heavy halter rope in O'Rourke's other hand curl towards her head.

Hooves drummed down the hillside from the church. Ponies snorted and thundered towards the field.

The farmer's aim with the rope was good. In spite of Rosie's flailing hooves and angry cries, he managed to snake the rope through the air and over her head. He pulled the noose tight and leaned on the rope with all his weight as the frightened pony pulled away.

'Stop!' Mandy cried. She looked around as the rest of the herd galloped nearer.

The first pony took a soaring jump and cleared the hedge by the gate. It was the dun mare, coming to answer Rosie and Mandy's calls. She was in O'Rourke's field, mane and tail streaming behind her, leading the charge.

Another pony followed, then another; a white stallion and a grey mare. Their heels caught on the top branches of the hedge and sent leaves and flowers scattering on to the grass. Soon the field was full of stampeding wild ponies.

But O'Rourke was stubborn. He held on, dragged Rosie to the ground with the choking halter rope. Connie cowered by the cliff, confused by the shouts and squeals, thrusting out her head and calling for her mother.

Mandy and James ran for the gate. They had to get into the field and lead the foal away from the dangerous edge. They eased past the Land-rover and trailer waiting in the entrance. Seconds ticked by, but at last they were in with the ponies, running over the dew-covered grass to save Connie.

'Watch out!' James yelled as another pony soared over the hedge and landed only a couple of metres from Mandy. The black pony kicked out with her heels, making Mandy swerve and overbalance. This was a real stampede; the ponies were confused and frightened as they charged across Mandy and James's paths.

Then another figure came running and yelling through the gate towards them. He ignored the danger, heading straight for O'Rourke and Rosie.

'Sean!' Mandy gasped and got up from the ground. She began to run again. 'What are you doing here?' He was supposed to be in Galway, miles from here.

'Causing a stampede; what does it look like?' he yelled back. He drove the ponies towards the farmer, arms raised, pushing them on. His face was pale and drawn in the morning mist, his dark hair wet with dew. 'You didn't think I was going to let them take Rosie, did you?'

James caught up with Mandy. 'Come on, let's all work together!' he cried. 'Sean, what do you want us to do?'

'Work the ponies towards O'Rourke,' the boy muttered. 'We have to make him drop the rope!'

'Stay back!' The farmer saw them out of the corner of his eye. He raised the whip. 'I'll thrash the mare if you come any closer!'

Rosie snatched her head away, almost jerking her attacker off his feet. The black and grey ponies rushed past, almost shunting against O'Rourke, kicking out with their back legs. Bodies whirled and turned, hooves thudded on to the ground.

'Go ahead; try!' Sean called his bluff. He knew the mare was stronger than the man, and she was desperate.

O'Rourke raised the whip. Mandy saw it flick back through the air. But before he could bring it forward, Rosie pulled again. The halter rope slithered in his grasp and burned his palm. There was a cry of pain, then Rosie was free.

She reared over the farmer. He was bending forward in agony, clutching his hand. In a split second she could have brought her deadly hooves down on his head. But instead, she veered off.

She galloped for her foal at the dizzying cliff edge.

By now the field was full of ponies, all tearing through the misty air with their shrill, neighing cries. They jostled together, then raced off in different directions.

'It worked!' James said to Sean. The ponies' stampede had brought confusion and Rosie had made good her escape. Even now, the mare was beginning to bring order back to the herd. Trailing the useless halter rope, she gathered Connie from the dangerous cliff and made her stay by her side. Then she reared and called for the others to gather in the far corner of the field.

'Not yet, it didn't!' O'Rourke ran towards Sean, still clutching his whip. He was coming to his senses, beginning to realise what had happened. 'You're out of your mind, boy!' he yelled at Sean.

Sean faced him. He didn't say a word, but the look on his face told the farmer that he didn't care. O'Rourke could do and say what he liked; it would make no difference. Rosie was still free.

The man raised his whip and brought it down so close to Sean that it ruffled his hair. The boy still didn't flinch. O'Rourke shouted again. 'Wait till I tell your father!'

Mandy and James stepped forward. The farmer

was about to raise his whip once more. Then he stopped. He lunged forward instead and grabbed Sean by the arm. 'I won't have them locking me up for teaching you a lesson!' he snarled. 'I've got a better idea!'

Mandy saw that he was strong; much taller and heavier than Sean. Though their friend struggled, he couldn't stop O'Rourke from wrapping his arms round his chest and lifting him clean off the ground. Then he dragged him, fighting and kicking, towards his Land-rover.

'Where are you taking him?' James ran after them, trying to pull Sean from the farmer's grasp. The boy had gone limp. Dazed and winded, he looked as if all the fight had gone out of him.

'To Lough Caher!' came the snarling reply as O'Rourke pulled the gate closed behind him. 'Do what you like! Say what you like! But just remember; you haven't a shred of evidence. No one will believe a word you say!'

Ten

The farmer shoved Sean into the Land-rover, locked him in and unhitched the trailer. Then he raced away in the Land-rover, leaving the un-hitched trailer blocking the gate.

Mandy took stock; the field was swarming with a dozen or more stampeding ponies and there was no way out.

'James, go and get help!' she cried. 'Ask Mum and Dad to fetch Molloy. We've got to move that trailer away from the gate and set the ponies free!'

James drew breath, then nodded. 'What about you?'

'I'll stay and keep an eye on Rosie and Connie.' She glanced at the mare and foal. Rosie dragged the long halter rope along the ground after her as she nudged at Connie.

So James climbed over the gate and ran up the hill towards the ruined church. Soon the mist swallowed him and Mandy was left alone with the frightened animals.

She turned full circle, wondering what to do. Hedges loomed on three sides. On the fourth, there was the deadly drop to the beach below. The ponies had bunched together and were running as a herd; except for Rosie and Connie, who stood apart.

Then, as Mandy struggled to find an answer and waited for James to fetch help, she saw the young, adventurous grey pony come to the head of the bunch and take the lead. He steered a course round the rim of the field, skimming the hedges. Then suddenly, he changed direction, charging across the middle, close to where Mandy stood. To a barrage of snorts and stamps, he led the herd.

The grey Connemara pony flew towards the barrier. Surefooted on the dew-sodden grass, he went at the hedge and soared into the air. He jumped clear, followed one by one by the other graceful, plucky members of the herd.

'Above all, they have a reputation for being excellent jumpers.' Mandy allowed herself a faint smile as she recalled her dad's words. These beautiful ponies were clever and hardy. And they'd just proved to her that they could jump anything that got in their way.

But that left Rosie and Connie alone in the field. The mare had refused to take her place at the front of the fleeing herd, knowing that her foal was too small to leap the hedge. Instead, full of suspicion towards Mandy, she trotted the young pony into a far corner and stamped her feet in warning.

'It's OK.' Mandy approached slowly. After what O'Rourke had tried to do, she could hardly blame Rosie for not trusting her any more. 'I won't hurt you,' she whispered gently.

But Rosie reared and warned her off. Connie cowered against the hedge.

Mandy halted in the middle of the field. Maybe . . . She frowned as she tried to remember exactly what Sean would do now.

Maybe . . . maybe she could talk to Rosie, as Sean would have done! He would square up to her, hands raised, fingers outspread. Mandy tried it, staring Rosie in the eye.

Startled, the mare retreated, taking Connie with her. She began to canter rapidly round the rim of the field, as Mandy challenged and pressed her.

She's fleeing! Mandy thought. This was right. This was what was meant to happen. The mare should want to get away, but the hedges held her trapped. She should run five or six times around the perimeter, watching, listening.

Mandy said nothing. She spoke with gestures and looks. Soon Rosie's ear locked on to her, recognising her authority. *OK, keep on running away*! Mandy thought. *Look at me. Listen to me. I'll tell you when I'm ready to do a deal*!

Deep inside, she was afraid that what she was attempting might not work, but she wouldn't let Rosie see this. Outwardly she was calm, keeping her hands raised, her body square on to the mare and her foal.

Right, now your head should go down! Mandy's gaze was locked on to Rosie's eyes. She waited for the signal to say that the mare had given in.

On the sixth circuit of the field, Rosie's head went down.

It was time for Mandy to copy Sean's next move

from when she'd seen him working in the training arena. Now she must turn away from confrontation, hold her body at a forty-five degree angle to the mare, lower her gaze.

Straight away Rosie stopped. She tucked Connie behind her and took a step towards Mandy.

It's working! Mandy kept calm, though her heart raced. *Keep on coming! Come on*! She prayed for Rosie to approach her.

The mare walked on with Connie. She came without hesitating to within centimetres of where Mandy stood.

Don't frighten her. Don't look her in the eye! Mandy remembered the basic rule. Slowly, easily, she reached up to rub the blind spot between Rosie's eyes. *I'm on your side*! she promised, without speaking a word.

Mandy felt Rosie's dappled flanks quiver as she moved her hand softly over her neck and shoulders. Almost without noticing, she took hold of the trailing halter rope and turned to lead the mare towards the blocked gate.

'Good girl!' For the first time she spoke out loud. She knew that Connie would stay tucked in behind them as they made for the gate. And now she could hear a car coming across country from the direction of the church.

Thank you, James! She steadied Rosie and walked on. He'd fetched help. Her mum and dad, perhaps Molloy and other villagers, would be able to shift the trailer from the entrance to the field. They would open the gate. She would be able to lead Rosie and Connie out, take off the halter and set them free.

But it was Gerry Malone's red Land-rover that came speeding through the mist, with two other figures inside. Mandy had time to make out Tom O'Rourke and Sean, before the two men leaped from the car and strode towards the gate.

Fear flooded through Mandy. It spread to Rosie and Connie. The mare dug in her heels and refused to budge. Her nostrils flared wide, she laid her ears flat against her sweating neck.

'Stop where you are. You're not taking that mare anywhere!' Malone warned as he stood by the trailer.

O'Rourke went to work and crashed the trailer ramp down. The sound went through every nerve in Mandy's body. The trailer stood open, waiting for Rosie and Connie.

But instead, another car arrived. O'Rourke and Malone heard it and scrambled back towards the

Land-rover. In the confusion Sean seized his chance. Jumping from his father's car, he ran and seized the ramp to the farmer's trailer, lifted it and rammed the bolts back into place.

'Thank you!' Mandy breathed, closing her eyes.

When she opened them again, she saw James reach the gate. Then her mum and dad arrived with Molloy. They put their weight behind the trailer and began to shove. Slowly they edged it clear of the gate.

Carefully, quietly, Sean opened the gate and stepped into the field. Not once did he look Rosie in the eye as he approached Mandy and stood by her side. 'You did it!' he whispered with a smile.

Holding her head high, steadying Rosie, she nodded. 'I did what you do. I talked to her!' she agreed.

Molloy collared O'Rourke and Gerry Malone before they could drive off. He stood demanding an explanation, while she, James and Sean gave the full story to Emily and Adam Hope.

'You know what was even better than getting Rosie to trust me?' Mandy said to her mum and dad.

They were walking towards the church as the

morning mist cleared from the point and gave them the first glimpse of the sun shining on green fields and distant purple mountains.

'Setting her and Connie loose,' Emily Hope murmured, relieved that the dangerous situation had worked out well in the end.

Mandy sighed and nodded. 'I'll never forget the look on Rosie's face when I slipped the halter off!'

The mare had dipped her head and nudged Mandy's hand with her velvety muzzle. The gate swung open. Nothing stood between her and freedom.

'You did well to catch her in the first place,' Adam Hope told her. 'According to James, there was a fair amount of panic going on in that field.'

'All thanks to Sean,' Mandy insisted. 'I remembered what he did, and copied every single movement!'

'You hear that?' Adam turned to a glowering Gerry Malone. 'Sean's system works. Mandy just proved it beyond a shadow of a doubt!'

'He's a talented boy,' Molloy agreed, urging the trainer and the farmer up the hill to join Mandy's group. 'I'd say it was time to admit your mistakes, Gerry, and face the facts. This lad of yours has a way with the horses, and no mistake!'

Adam grinned at Emily, James and Mandy, as Sean reddened to hear his own praises sung out loud.

Gerry Malone grimaced and frowned. He turned this way and that as the shopkeeper lectured him.

'Now, we all know you have your own tried and tested ways,' Molloy went on, ignoring the much taller figure of O'Rourke hovering behind him. He concentrated for the moment on bringing the trainer to task for the shady business which the shopkeeper had evidently long suspected.

'And, Gerry, we respect you here in Drumcashel for the horses you turn out on the racetracks for miles around. They're always the best-looking horses on the course. But . . .'

Molloy rolled his eyes and said 'But . . .' in a way that was full of meaning. 'People talk, you know. There have been rumours that you've had a hand in the mysterious disappearance of one or two wild ponies in the not too distant past.' He raised a hand to prevent the trainer from rushing in, restraining his obvious disgust at what Malone had done. 'Of course, we don't pay a lot of attention to wild stories like that.'

Mandy stole another look at Sean. No wonder the boy had practically lived on the clifftop, keeping an eye on Rosie's herd! He must have known his father and O'Rourke's guilty secret after all. Yet he hadn't been able to say a word to stop it without landing his own father in serious trouble. Now he stared at his feet while the shopkeeper laid his final card on the table.

'I heard people say just yesterday that they were certain the horse thieves have already moved away from Drumcashel.' Molloy's clear grey eyes looked directly from Gerry Malone to Tom O'Rourke. He ignored the trailer in the gateway to the field and the culprits' guilty looks.

Instead, he fixed a meaningful gaze on them both and spoke slowly and forcefully. 'We're quite sure in our own minds that there'll be no more wild ponies disappearing from the national park.'

Gerry Malone gave a huge sigh of relief. 'Thanks, Molloy. If there's anything I can do . . .'

'You can swallow your pride over your boy's brilliant training method for a start,' the wise shopkeeper insisted. He waited for a full apology.

The proud trainer struggled with his conscience. 'I suppose there's always room for new methods,' he said at last. For the first time that

morning he looked Sean full in the face. 'Sometimes it's hard for a father to accept that his son is
catching him up, even overtaking him,' he told
him quietly. 'But it looks like that's what I have to
do.'

Sean swallowed hard and nodded. Tears welled
up in his clear grey eyes.

Molloy slapped Sean on the back, wanting to
show everyone that he had complete faith in him.
'I wouldn't be surprised if the lad is ready to set
up his own training yard in a few years' time. You'll
have a big rival there, that's for sure!'

Gerry Malone nodded. He'd learned his lesson.
'Sean can work on his method whenever he comes
home to Lough Caher. I'll be interested to see
how it develops.'

'That's great.' Emily Hope smiled at Mandy.

'That's more than great. That's brilliant!' Molloy
crowed. 'You've had a fair promise from your dad,
Sean. And don't you worry, I'll be over next week
to see how you're getting along!'

Mandy nodded with satisfaction, and was glad
to hear her own father step in and make his point.

'I'd count myself lucky if I were you,' he told
the trainer and the ruthless farmer. 'Back home
at Animal Ark, we always take this kind of cruelty

to ponies very seriously. It would mean a court case and a stiff fine at the very least.' He looked sternly from Malone to O'Rourke. 'I can understand that money worries put a lot of pressure on people, but I'd never let that be an excuse for cruelty to animals.'

James and Mrs Hope stood beside Mandy, fiercely but silently agreeing with Adam Hope. Mandy saw O'Rourke bite his lip and give a stubborn shake of his head. She wondered what Molloy had lined up for the farmer by way of punishment. *He shouldn't get off scot-free*, she thought.

'But on this occasion, we're saying that this can be the end of the whole matter,' Molloy confirmed to Gerry Malone.

'If Molloy stood for president, I'd vote for him!' Adam Hope said with a laugh.

Mandy and James had spent the sunny day rowing a curragh into narrow coves and out to the rocky islands off Drumcashel beach.

'Why? What's he done now?' Mandy rubbed salt water from her legs with the towel that her mum handed to her.

'Have a piece of cake and a drink, James.' Emily

Hope had brought them a treat on to the beach. 'This will keep you going until later this evening. We're having supper in the village, courtesy of Molloy. He's offered us all a free meal!'

'Is that why you'd vote for him, Dad?' Mandy grinned.

Adam Hope paddled in the shallow waves, wincing as the cold water washed around his ankles. 'There's that, and the fact that he's a born politician. Did you see how he handled Gerry Malone this morning?'

Mandy smiled and nodded. Thanks to Molloy, Sean was safe to go on working in his own way with the horses at Lough Caher. 'Anything else?'

'Well, now we hear how he plans to deal with Tom O'Rourke!' Emily Hope took over.

'. . . By sending him into exile!' Adam said with a grin.

James bit into his chocolate cake and gave Mandy a puzzled shrug.

'. . . By making him an outcast from the village!' Emily added.

'. . . He's banned him from Molloys!' Adam explained. 'Believe me, if you live here in Drumcashel, that's the worst punishment you can possibly imagine!'

* * *

The ponies came at sunset. Mandy and James had stayed on the beach after Mandy's mum and dad had gone up to the cottage.

Rosie led the way down the cliff path, ahead of Connie and the rest. They came in single file on to the smooth sands, then gathered by the water's edge.

Mandy noticed the rebel grey venture further into the water and smiled when Rosie went to round him up. The low sun made Connie's chestnut coat glow.

Then Rosie set off for Kilmore Cove, leading the herd. She trotted through the shallow waves, raising white foam, breaking into a canter and then into a wide, easy gallop. Little Connie strode out gallantly to keep up with her mother. Her

awkward foal's legs pranced and kicked. Soon twenty ponies picked up speed and charged through the spray.

'Do you think they saw us?' James whispered. He stood up from the warm rock where he'd been sitting.

Mandy nodded. She was happy to stay where she was, watching the herd from a distance. It was as it should be; the ponies wary and watchful, galloping free.

ANIMAL ARK

Lucy Daniels

All Hodder Children's books are available at your local bookshop, or can be ordered direct from the publisher. Just tick the titles you would like and complete the details below. Prices and availability are subject to change without prior notice.

Please enclose a cheque or postal order made payable to *Bookpoint Ltd*, and send to: Hodder Children's Books, 39 Milton Park, Abingdon, OXON OX14 4TD, UK. Email Address: orders@bookpoint.co.uk

If you would prefer to pay by credit card, our call centre team would be delighted to take your order by telephone. Our direct line *01235 400414* (lines open 9.00 am–6.00 pm Monday to Saturday, 24 hour message answering service). Alternatively you can send a fax on *01235 400454*.

TITLE	FIRST NAME		SURNAME	

ADDRESS	
DAYTIME TEL:	POST CODE

If you would prefer to pay by credit card, please complete: Please debit my Visa/Access/Diner's Card/American Express (delete as applicable) card no:

Signature ....

Expiry Date: ....

If you would NOT like to receive further information on our products please tick the box. ❏

JESS THE BORDER COLLIE
Lucy Daniels

Her brand new series!

0 340 70438 1	The Arrival	£3.99	❏
0 340 70439 X	The Challenge	£3.99	❏
0 340 70440 3	The Runaway	£3.99	❏

All Hodder Children's books are available at your local bookshop, or can be ordered direct from the publisher. Just tick the titles you would like and complete the details below. Prices and availability are subject to change without prior notice.

Please enclose a cheque or postal order made payable to *Bookpoint Ltd*, and send to: Hodder Children's Books, 39 Milton Park, Abingdon, OXON OX14 4TD, UK.
Email Address: orders@bookpoint.co.uk

If you would prefer to pay by credit card, our call centre team would be delighted to take your order by telephone. Our direct line *01235 400414* (lines open 9.00 am–6.00 pm Monday to Saturday, 24 hour message answering service). Alternatively you can send a fax on *01235 400454*.

TITLE		FIRST NAME		SURNAME	

ADDRESS	

DAYTIME TEL:		POST CODE	

If you would prefer to pay by credit card, please complete:
Please debit my Visa/Access/Diner's Card/American Express (delete as applicable) card no:

Signature .... Expiry Date: ....

If you would NOT like to receive further information on our products please tick the box. ❏

ANIMAL ACTION

If you like *Animal Ark* then you'll love the RSPCA's Animal Action Club! Anyone aged 13 or under can become a member for just £5.50 a year. Join up and you can look forward to six issues of Animal Action magazine - each one is bursting with animal news, competitions, features, posters and celebrity interviews. Plus we'll send you a fantastic joining pack too!

To be really animal-friendly just complete the form – a photocopy is fine – and send it, with a cheque or postal order for £5.50

 (made payable to the RSPCA), to Animal Action Club, RSPCA, Causeway, Horsham, West Sussex RH12 1HG. We'll then send you a joining pack and your first copy of *Animal Action*.

Registered charity no 219099

Don't delay, join today!

Name ....

Address ....

....

Postcode

....

Date of birth ....

Youth membership of the Royal Society for the Prevention of Cruelty to Animals

AACHOD2